THE STORE BOY

HORATIO ALGER, Jr.

1st WORLD
LIBRARY
Literary Society

The Store Boy

Horatio Alger, Jr.

© 1st World Library – Literary Society, 2004
PO Box 2211
Fairfield, IA 52556
www.1stworldlibrary.org
First Edition

LCCN: 2004091216

Softcover ISBN: 1-59540-654-9
eBook ISBN: 1-59540-754-5

Purchase *"The Store Boy"*
as a traditional bound book at:
www.1stWorldLibrary.org/purchase.asp?ISBN=1-59540-654-9

1st World Library Literary Society is a nonprofit organization dedicated to promoting literacy by:

- Creating a free internet library accessible from any computer worldwide.
- Hosting writing competitions and offering book publishing scholarships.

Readers interested in supporting literacy through sponsorship, donations or membership please contact:
literacy@1stworldlibrary.org
Check us out at: www.1stworldlibrary.org

The Store Boy
contributed by the Mahaney Family
in support of
1st World Library Literary Society

CHAPTER I

BEN BARCLAY MEETS A TRAMP

"Give me a ride?"

Ben Barclay checked the horse he was driving and looked attentively at the speaker. He was a stout-built, dark-complexioned man, with a beard of a week's growth, wearing an old and dirty suit, which would have reduced any tailor to despair if taken to him for cleaning and repairs. A loose hat, with a torn crown, surmounted a singularly ill-favored visage.

"A tramp, and a hard looking one!" said Ben to himself.

He hesitated about answering, being naturally reluctant to have such a traveling companion.

"Well, what do you say?" demanded the tramp rather impatiently. "There's plenty of room on that seat, and I'm dead tired."

"Where are you going?" asked Ben.

"Same way you are - to Pentonville."

"You can ride," said Ben, in a tone by means cordial,

and he halted his horse till his unsavory companion climbed into the wagon.

They were two miles from Pentonville, and Ben had a prospect of a longer ride than he desired under the circumstances. His companion pulled out a dirty clay pipe from his pocket, and filled it with tobacco, and then explored another pocket for a match. A muttered oath showed that he failed to find one.

"Got a match, boy?" he asked.

"No," answered Ben, glad to have escaped the offensive fumes of the pipe.

"Just my luck!" growled the tramp, putting back the pipe with a look of disappointment. "If you had a match now, I wouldn't mind letting you have a whiff or two.

"I don't smoke," answered Ben, hardly able to repress a look of disgust.

"So you're a good boy, eh? One of the Sunday school kids that want to be an angel, hey? Pah!" and the tramp exhibited the disgust which the idea gave him.

"Yes, I go to Sunday school," said Ben coldly, feeling more and more repelled by his companion.

"I never went to Sunday school," said his companion. "And I wouldn't. It's only good for milksops and hypocrites."

"Do you think you're any better for not going?" Ben couldn't help asking.

"I haven't been so prosperous, if that's what you mean. I'm a straightforward man, I am. You always know where to find me. There ain't no piety about me. What are you laughin' at?"

"No offense," said Ben. "I believe every word you say."

"You'd better. I don't allow no man to doubt my word, nor no boy, either. Have you got a quarter about you?"

"No."

"Nor a dime? A dime'll do."

"I have no money to spare."

"I'd pay yer to-morrer."

"You'll have to borrow elsewhere; I am working in a store for a very smell salary, and that I pay over to my mother."

"Whose store?"

"Simon Crawford's; but you won't know any better for my telling you that, unless you are acquainted in Pentonville"

"I've been through there. Crawford keeps the grocery store."

"Yes."

"What's your name?"

"Ben Barclay," answered our hero, feeling rather annoyed at what he considered intrusive curiosity.

"Barclay?" replied the tramp quickly. "Not John Barclay's son?"

It was Ben's turn to be surprised. He was the son of John Barclay, deceased, but how could his ill-favored traveling companion know that?

"Did you know my father?" asked the boy, astonished.

"I've heerd his name," answered the tramp, in an evasive tone.

"What is your name?" asked Ben, feeling that be had a right to be as curious as his companion.

"I haven't got any visitin' cards with me," answered the tramp dryly.

"Nor I; but I told you my name."

"All right; I'll tell you mine. You can call me Jack Frost."

"I gave you my real name," said Ben significantly.

"I've almost forgotten what my real name is," said the tramp. "If you don't like Jack Frost, you can call me George Washington."

Ben laughed.

"I don't think that name would suit, he said. George Washington never told a lie."

"What d'ye mean by that?" demanded the tramp, his brow darkening.

"I was joking," answered Ben, who did not care to get into difficulty with such a man.

"I'm going to joke a little myself," growled the tramp, as, looking quickly about him, he observed that they were riding over a lonely section of the road lined with woods. "Have you got any money about you?"

Ben, taken by surprise, would have been glad to answer "No," but he was a boy of truth, and could not say so truly, though he might have felt justified in doing so under the circumstances.

"Come, I see you have. Give it to me right off or it'll be worse for you."

Now it happened that Ben had not less than twenty-five dollars about him. He had carried some groceries to a remote part of the town, and collected two bills on the way. All this money he had in a wallet in the pocket on the other side from the tramp. But the money was not his; it belonged to his employer, and he was not disposed to give it up without a struggle; though he knew that in point of strength he was not an equal match for the man beside him.

"You will get no money from me," he answered in a firm tone, though be felt far from comfortable.

"I won't, hey!" growled the tramp. "D'ye think I'm goin' to let a boy like you get the best of me?"

He clutched Ben by the arm, and seemed in a fair way

to overcome opposition by superior strength, when a fortunate idea struck Ben. In his vest pocket was a silver dollar, which had been taken at the store, but proving to be counterfeit, had been given to Ben by Mr. Crawford as a curiosity.

This Ben extracted from his pocket, and flung out by the roadside.

"If you want it, you'll have to get out and get it," he said.

The tramp saw the coin glistening upon the ground, and had no suspicion of its not being genuine. It was not much - only a dollar - but he was "dead broke," and it was worth picking up. He had not expected that Ben had much, and so was not disappointed.

"Curse you!" he said, relinquishing his hold upon Ben. "Why couldn't you give it to me instead of throwing it out there?"

"Because," answered Ben boldly, "I didn't want you to have it."

"Get out and get it for me!"

"I won't!" answered Ben firmly.

"Then stop the horse and give me a chance to get out."

"I'll do that."

Ben brought the horse to a halt, and his unwelcome passenger descended, much to his relief. He had to walk around the wagon to get at the coin. Our hero brought down the whip with emphasis on the horse's back and the animal dashed off at a good rate of speed.

"Stop!" exclaimed the tramp, but Ben had no mind to heed his call.

"No, my friend, you don't get another chance to ride with me," he said to himself.

The tramp picked up the coin, and his practiced eye detected that it was bogus.

"The young villain!" he muttered angrily. "I'd like to wring his neck. It's a bad one after all." He looked after the receding team and was half disposed to follow, but he changed his mind, reflecting, "I can pass it anyhow."

Instead of pursuing his journey, he made his way into the woods, and, stretching himself out among the underbrush, went to sleep.

Half a mile before reaching the store, Ben overtook Rose Gardiner, who had the reputation of being the prettiest girl in Pendleton - at any rate, such was Ben's opinion. She looked up and smiled pleasantly at Ben as he took off his hat.

"Shall you attend Prof. Harrington's entertainment at the Town Hall this evening, Ben?" she asked, after they had interchanged greetings.

"I should like to go," answered Ben, "but I am afraid I can't be spared from the store. Shall you go?"

"I wouldn't miss it for anything. I hope I shall see

you there."

"I shall want to go all the more then." answered Ben gallantly.

"You say that to flatter me," said the young lady, with an arch smile.

"No, I don't," said Ben earnestly. "Won't you get in and ride as far as the store?"

"Would it be proper?" asked Miss Rose demurely.

"Of course it would."

"Then I'll venture."

Ben jumped from the wagon, assisted the young lady in, and the two drove into the village together. He liked his second passenger considerably better than the first.

Horatio Alger, Jr.

CHAPTER II

BEN AND HIS MOTHER

Ben Barclay, after taking leave of the tramp, lost no time in driving to the grocery store where he was employed. It was a large country store, devoted not to groceries alone, but supplies of dry-goods, boots and shoes, and the leading articles required in the community. There were two other clerks besides Ben, one the son, another the nephew, of Simon Crawford, the proprietor.

"Did you collect any money, Ben?" asked Simon, who chanced to be standing at the door when our hero drove up.

"Yes, sir; I collected twenty-five dollars, but came near losing it on the way home."

"How was that? I hope you were not careless."

"No, except in taking a stranger as a passenger. When we got to that piece of woods a mile back, he asked me for all the money I had."

"A highwayman, and so near Pentonville!" ejaculated Simon Crawford. "What was he like?"

"A regular tramp."

"Yet you say you have the money. How did you manage to keep it from him?"

Ben detailed the stratagem of which he made use.

"You did well," said the storekeeper approvingly. "I must give you a dollar for the one you sacrificed."

"But sir, it was bad money. I couldn't have passed it."

"That does not matter. You are entitled to some reward for the courage and quick wit you displayed. Here is a dollar, and - let me see, there is an entertainment at the Town Hall this evening, isn't there?"

"Yes, sir. Prof. Harrington, the magician, gives an entertainment," said Ben eagerly.

"At what time does it commence?"

"At eight o'clock."

"You may leave the store at half-past seven. That will give you enough time to get there."

"Thank you, sir. I wanted to go to the entertainment, but did not like to ask for the evening."

"You have earned it. Here is the dollar," and Mr. Crawford handed the money to his young clerk, who received it gratefully.

A magical entertainment may be a very common affair to my young readers in the city, but in a country village it is an event. Pentonville was too small to have any regular place of amusement, and its citizens were obliged to depend upon traveling performers, who, from time to time, engaged the Town Hall. Some time had elapsed since there had been any such entertainment, and Prof. Harrington was the more likely to be well patronized. Ben, who had the love of amusement common to boys of his age, had been regretting the necessity of remaining in the store till nine o'clock, and therefore losing his share of amusement when, as we have seen, an opportunity suddenly offered.

"I am glad I met the tramp, after all," he said to himself. "He has brought me luck."

At supper he told is mother what had befallen him, but she tool a more serious view of it than he did.

"He might have murdered you, Ben," she said with a shudder.

"Oh, no; he wouldn't do that. He might have stolen Mr. Crawford's money; that was the most that was likely to happen."

"I didn't think there were highwaymen about here. Now I shall be worrying about you."

"Don't do that mother; I don't feel in any danger. Still, if you think it best, I will carry a pistol."

"No, no, Ben! it might go off and kill you. I would rather run the risk of a highwayman. I wonder if the man is prowling about in the neighborhood yet?"

"I don't think my bogus dollar will carry him very far.

By the way, mother, I must tell yon one strange thing. He asked me if I was John Barclay's son."

"What!" exclaimed Mrs. Barclay, in a tone of great surprise. "Did he know your name was Barclay?"

"Not till I told him. Then it was he asked if I was the son of John Barclay."

"Did he say he knew your father?"

"I asked him, but he answered evasively."

"He might have seen some resemblance - that is, if he had ever met your father. Ah! it was a sad day for us all when your poor father died. We should have been in a very different position," the widow sighed.

"Yes, mother," said Ben; "but when I get older I will try to supply my father's place, and relieve you from care and trouble."

"You are doing that in a measure now, my dear boy," said Mrs. Barclay affectionately. "You are a great comfort to me."

Ben's answer was to go up to his mother and kiss her. Some boys of his age are ashamed to show their love for the mother who is devoted to them, but it a false shame, that does them no credit.

"Still, mother, you work too hard," said Ben. "Wait till I am a man, and you shall not need to work at all."

Mrs. Barclay had been a widow for five years. Her husband had been a commercial traveler, but had contracted a fever at Chicago, and died after a brief illness, without his wife having the satisfaction of ministering to him in his last days. A small sum due him from his employers was paid over to his family, but no property was discovered, though his wife had been under the impression that her husband possessed some. He had never been in the habit of confiding his business affairs to her, and so, if he had investments of any kind, she could not learn anything about them. She found herself, therefore, with no property except a small cottage, worth, with its quarter acre of land, perhaps fifteen hundred dollars. As Ben was too small to earn anything, she had been compelled to raise about seven hundred dollars on mortgage, which by this time had been expended for living. Now, Ben was earning four dollars a week, and, with her own earnings, she was able to make both ends meet without further encroachments upon her scanty property; but the mortgage was a source of anxiety to her, especially as it was held by Squire Davenport, a lawyer of considerable means, who was not overscrupulous about the methods by which he strove to increase his hoards. Should he at any time take it into his head to foreclose, there was no one to whom Mrs. Barclay could apply to assume the mortgage, and she was likely to be compelled to sacrifice her home. He had more than once hinted that he might need the money but as yet had gone no further.

Mrs. Barclay had one comfort, however, and a great one. This was a good son. Ben was always kind to his mother - a bright, popular, promising boy - and though at present he was unable to earn much, in a few years he would be able to earn a good income, and then his mother knew that she would be well provided for. So she did not allow herself to borrow trouble but looked forward hopefully, thanking God for what He had given her.

"Won't you go up to the Town Hall with me, mother?" asked Ben. I am sure you would enjoy it."

"Thank you, Ben, for wishing me to have a share in your amusements," his mother replied, "but I have a little headache this evening, and I shall be better off at home."

"It isn't on account of the expense you decline, mother, is it? You know Mr. Crawford gave me a dollar, and the tickets are but twenty-five cents."

"No, it isn't that, Ben. If it were a concert I might be tempted to go in spite of my headache, but a magical entertainment would not amuse me as much as it will you."

"Just as you think best, mother; but I should like to have you go. You won't feel lonely, will you?"

"I am used to being alone till nine o'clock, when you are at the store."

This conversation took place at the supper table. Ben went directly from the store to the Town Hall, where he enjoyed himself as much as he anticipated. If he could have foreseen how his mother was to pass that evening, it would have destroyed all is enjoyment.

CHAPTER III

MRS. BARCLAY'S CALLERS

About half-past eight o'clock Mrs. Barclay sat with her work in her hand. Her headache was better, but she did not regret not having accompanied Ben to the Town Hall.

"I am glad Ben is enjoying himself," she thought, "but I would rather stay quietly at home. Poor boy! he works hard enough, and needs recreation now and then."

Just then a knock was heard at the outside door.

"I wonder who it can be?" thought the widow. "I supposed everybody would be at the Town Hall. It may be Mrs. Perkins come to borrow something."

Mrs. Perkins was a neighbor much addicted to borrowing, which was rather disagreeable, but might have been more easily tolerated but that she seldom returned the articles lent.

Mrs. Barclay went to the door and opened it, fully expecting to see her borrowing neighbor. A very different person met her view. The ragged hat, the ill-looking face, the neglected attire, led her to recognize the tramp whom Ben had described to her as having attempted to rob him in the afternoon. Terrified, Mrs. Barclay's first impulse was to shut the door and bolt it. But her unwelcome visitor was too quick for her. Thrusting his foot into the doorway, he interposed an effectual obstacle in the way of shutting the door.

"No, you don't, ma'am!" he said, with as laugh. "I understand your little game. You want to shut me out."

"What do you want?" asked the widow apprehensively.

"What do I want?" returned the tramp. "Well, to begin with, I want something to eat - and drink," he added, after a pause.

"Why don't you go to the tavern?" asked Mrs. Barclay, anxious for him to depart.

"Well, I can't afford it. All the money I've got is a bogus dollar your rogue of a son gave me this afternoon."

"You stole it from him," said the widow indignantly.

"What's the odds if I did. It ain't of no value. Come, haven't you anything to eat in the house? I'm hungry as a wolf."

"And you look like one!" thought Mrs. Barclay, glancing at his unattractive features; but she did not dare to say it.

There seemed no way of refusing, and she was glad to comply with his request, if by so doing she could soon get rid of him.

Horatio Alger, Jr.

"Stay here," she said, "and I'll bring you some bread and butter and cold meat."

"Thank you, I'd rather come in," said the tramp, and he pushed his way through the partly open door.

She led the way uneasily into the kitchen just in the rear of the sitting room where she had been seated.

"I wish Ben was here," she said to herself, with sinking heart.

The tramp seated himself at the kitchen table, while Mrs. Barclay, going to the pantry, brought out part of a loaf of bread, and butter, and a few slices of cold beef, which she set before him. Without ceremony he attacked the viands and ate as if half famished. When about half through, he turned to the widow, and asked:

"Haven't you some whisky in the house?"

"I never keep any," answered Mrs. Barclay.

"Rum or gin, then?" I ain't partic'lar. I want something to warm me up."

"I keep no liquor of any kind. I don't approve of drink, or want Ben to touch it."

"Oh, you belong to the cold water army, do you?" said the tramp with a sneer. "Give me some coffee, then."

"I have no fire, and cannot prepare any."

"What have you got, then?" demanded than unwelcome guest impatiently.

"I can give you a glass of excellent well water."

"[illegible] Do you want to choke me?" returned the tramp in disgust.

"Suppose I mix you some molasses and water," suggested the widow, anxious to propitiate her dangerous guest.

"Humph! Well, that will do, if you've got nothing better. Be quick about it, for my throat is parched."

As soon as possible the drink was prepared and set beside his plate. He drained it at a draught, and called for a second glass, which was supplied him. Presently, for all things must have an end, the tramp's appetite seemed to be satisfied. He threw himself back in his chair, stretched his legs, and, with his hands in his pockets, fixed his eyes on the widow.

"I feel better," he said.

"I am glad to hear it," said Mrs. Barclay. "Now, if you'll be kind enough, leave the house, for I expect Ben back before long."

"And you don't want him to get hurt," laughed the tramp. "Well, I do owe him a flogging for a trick he played on me."

"Oh, pray, go away!" said Mrs. Barclay, apprehensively. "I have given you some supper, and that ought to satisfy you."

"I can't go away till I've talked to you a little on business."

"Business! What business can you have with me?"

"More than you think. You are the widow of John Barclay, ain't you?"

"Yes; did you know my husband?"

"Yes; that is, I saw something of him just before he died."

"Can you tell me anything about his last moments?" asked the widow, forgetting the character of her visitor, and only thinking of her husband.

"No, that isn't in my line. I ain't a doctor nor yet a minister. I say, did he leave any money?"

"Not that we have been able to find out. He owned this hone, but left no other property."

"That you know of," said the tramp, significantly.

"Do you know of any?" asked Mrs. Barclay eagerly. "How did you happen to know him?"

"I was the barkeeper in the hotel where he died. It was a small house, not one of your first-class hotels."

"My husband was always careful of his expenses. He did not spend money unnecessarily. With his prudence we all thought he must have some investments, but we could discover none."

"Have you got any money in the house?" asked the tramp, with seeming abruptness.

"Why do you ask?" returned the widow, alarmed. "Surely, you would not rob me?"

"No, I don't want to rob you. I want to sell you something."

"I don't care to buy. It takes all our money for necessary expenses."

"You don't ask what I have to sell."

"No, because I cannot buy it, whatever it may be."

"It is - a secret," said the tramp.

"A secret!" repeated Mrs. Barclay, bewildered.

"Yes, and a secret worth buying. Your husband wasn't so poor as you think. He left stock and papers representing three thousand dollars, and I am the only man who can put you in the way of getting it."

Mrs. Barclay was about to express her surprise, when a loud knock was head at the outer door.

"Who's that?" demanded the tramp quickly. "Is it the boy?"

"No, he would not knock."

"Then, let me get out of this," he said, leaping to his feet. "Isn't there a back door?"

"Yes, there it is."

He hurried to the door, unbolted it, and made his

escape into the open beyond the house, just as the knock was repeated.

Confused by what she had heard, and the strange conduct of her visitor, the widow took the lamp and went to the door. To her surprise she found on opening it, two visitors, in one of whom she recognized Squire Davenport, already referred to as holding a mortgage on her house. The other was a short, dark-complexioned man, who looked like a mechanic.

"Excuse me the lateness of my call, Mrs. Barclay," said the squire smoothly. "I come on important business. This is Mr. Kirk, a cousin of my wife."

"Walk in, gentlemen," said Mrs. Barclay.

"This is night of surprises," she thought to herself.

CHAPTER IV

UNPLEASANT BUSINESS

It was now nine o'clock, rather a late hour for callers in the country, and Mrs. Barclay waited not without curiosity to hear the nature of the business which had brought her two visitors at that time.

"Take seats, gentlemen," she said, with the courtesy habitual to her.

Squire Davenport, who was disposed to consider that he had a right to the best of everything, seated himself in the rocking-chair, and signed his companion to a cane chair beside him.

"Mr. Kirk," he commenced, "is thinking of coming to Pentonville to live."

"I am glad to hear it," said Mrs. Barclay politely. Perhaps she would not have said this if she had known what was coming next.

"He is a carpenter," continued the squire, "and, as we have none in the village except old Mr. Wade, who is superannuated, I think he will find enough to do to keep him busy."

"I should think so," assented the widow.

"If he does not, I can employ him a part of the time on my land."

"What has all this to do with me?" thought Mrs. Barclay.

She soon learned.

"Of course he will need a house," pursued the squire, "and as his family is small, he thinks this house will just suit him."

"But I don't wish to sell," said the widow hurriedly. "I need this house for Ben and myself."

"You could doubtless find other accommodations. I dare say you could hire a couple of rooms from Elnathan Perkins."

"I wouldn't live in that old shell," said Mrs. Barclay rather indignantly, "and I am sure Ben wouldn't."

"I apprehend Benjamin will have no voice in the matter," said Squire Davenport stiffly. "He is only a boy."

"He is my main support, and my main adviser," said Mrs. Barclay, with spirit, "and I shall not take any step which is disagreeable to him."

Mr. Kirk looked disappointed, but the squire gave him an assuring look, as the widow could see.

"Perhaps you may change your mind," said the squire

significantly. "I am under the impression that I hold a mortgage on this property."

"Yes, sir," assented Mrs. Barclay apprehensively.

"For the sum of seven hundred dollars, if I am not mistaken."

"Yes, sir."

"I shall have need of this money for other purposes, and will trouble you to take it up."

"I was to have three months' notice," said the widow, with a troubled look.

"I will give you three months' notice to-night," said the squire.

"I don't know where to raise the money," faltered Mrs. Barclay.

"Then you had better sell to my friend here. He will assume the mortgage and pay you three hundred dollars."

"But that will be only a thousand dollars for the place."

"A very fair price, in my opinion, Mrs. Barclay."

"I have always considered it worth fifteen hundred dollars," said the widow, very much disturbed.

"A fancy price, my dear madam; quite an absurd price, I assure you. What do you say, Kirk?"

"I quite agree with you, squire," said Kirk, in a strong, nasal tone. "But then, women don't know anything of business."

"I know that you and your cousin are trying to take advantage of my poverty," said Mrs. Barclay bitterly. "If you are a carpenter, why don't you build a house for yourself, instead of trying to deprive me of mine?"

"That's my business," said Kirk rudely.

"Mr. Kirk cannot spare the time to build at present," said the squire.

"Then why doesn't he hire rooms from Elnathan Perkins, as you just recommended to me?"

"They wouldn't suit him," said the squire curtly. "He has set his mind on this house."

"Squire Davenport," said Mrs. Barclay, in a softened voice, "I am sure you cannot understand what you ask of me when you seek to take my home and turn me adrift. Here I lived with my poor husband; here my boy was born. During my married life I have had no other home. It is a humble dwelling, but it has associations and charms for me which it can never have for no one else. Let Mr. Kirk see some other house and leave me undisturbed in mine."

"Humph!" said the squire, shrugging his shoulders; "you look upon the matter from a sentimental point of view. That is unwise. It is simply a matter of business. You speak of the house as yours. In reality, it is more mine than yours, for I have a major interest in it. Think over my proposal coolly, and you will see that you are unreasonable. Mr. Kirk may be induced to give you a little more - say three hundred and fifty dollars - over and above the mortgage, which, as I said before, he is willing assume."

"How does it happen that you are willing to let the mortgage remain, if he buys, when you want the money for other purposes?" asked the widow keenly.

"He is a near relative of my wife, and that makes the difference, I apprehend."

"Well, madam, what do you say?" asked Kirk briskly.

"I say this, that I will keep the house if I can."

"You needn't expect that I will relent," said the squire hastily.

"I do not, for I see there is no consideration in your heart for a poor widow; but I cannot help thinking that Providence will raise up some kind friend who will buy the mortgage, or in some other way will enable me to save my home."

You are acting very foolishly, Mrs. Barclay, as you will realize in time. I give you a week in which to change your mind. Till then my friend Kirk's offer stands good. After that I cannot promise. If the property sold at auction I shouldn't he surprised if it did not fetch more than the amount of my lien upon it."

"I will trust in Providence, Squire Davenport."

"Providence won't pay off your mortgage, ma'am," said Kirk, with a coarse laugh.

Mrs. Barclay did not answer. She saw that he was a man of coarse fiber and did not care to notice him.

"Come along, Kirk," said the squire. "I apprehend she will be all right after a while. Mrs. Barclay will see her own interest when she comes to reflect."

"Good-evening, ma'am," said Kirk.

Mrs. Barclay inclined her head slowly, but did not reply.

When the two had left the house she sank into a chair and gave herself to painful thoughts. She had known that Squire Davenport had the right to dispossess her, but had not supposed he would do so as long as she paid the interest regularly. In order to do this, she and Ben had made earnest efforts, and denied themselves all but the barest necessities. Thus far she had succeeded. The interest on seven hundred dollars at six per cent. had amounted to forty-two dollars, and this was a large sum to pay, but thus far they had always had it ready. That Squire Davenport, with his own handsome mansion, would fix covetous eyes on her little home, she had not anticipated, but it had come to pass.

As to raising seven hundred dollars to pay off the mortgage, or induce any capitalist to furnish it, she feared it would be quite impossible.

She anxiously waited for Ben's return from the Town Hall in order to consult with him.

CHAPTER V

PROFESSOR HARRINGTON'S ENTERTAINMENT

Meanwhile Ben Barclay was enjoying himself at Professor Harrington's entertainment. He was at the Town Hall fifteen minutes before the time, and secured a seat very near the stage, or, perhaps it will be more correct to say, the platform. He had scarcely taken his seat when, to his gratification, Rose Gardiner entered the hall and sat down beside him.

"Good-evening, Ben," she said pleasantly. "So you came, after all."

Ben's face flushed with pleasure, for Rose Gardiner was, as we have said, the prettiest girl in Pentonville, and for this reason, as well as for her agreeable manners, was an object of attraction to the boys, who, while too young to be in love, were not insensible to the charms of a pretty face. I may add that Rose was the niece of the Rev. Mr. Gardiner, the minister of the leading church in the village.

"Good-evening, Rose," responded Ben, who was too well acquainted with the young lady to address her more formally; "I am glad to be in such company."

"I wish I could return the compliment," answered

Rose, with a saucy smile.

"Don't be too severe," said Ben, "or you will hurt my feelings."

"That would be a pity, surely; but how do do you happen to get off this evening? I thought you spent your evenings at the store."

"So I do, generally, but I was excused this evening for a special reason," and then he told of his adventure with the tramp.

Rose listened with eager attention.

"Weren't you terribly frightened?" she asked.

"No," answered Ben, adding, with a smile: "Even if I had been, I shouldn't like to confess it."

"I should have been so frightened that I would have screamed," continued the young lady.

"I didn't think of that," said Ben, amused. "I'll remember it next time."

"Oh, now I know you are laughing at me. Tell me truly, weren't you frightened?"

"I was only afraid I would lose Mr. Crawford's money. The tramp was stronger than I, and could have taken it from me if he had known I had it."

"You tricked him nicely. Where did he go? Do you think he is still in town?"

"He went into the woods. I don't think he is in the village. He would be afraid of being arrested."

At that very moment the tramp was in Ben's kitchen, but of that Ben had no idea.

"I don't know what I should do if I met him," said Rose. "You see I came alone. Aunt couldn't come with me, and uncle, being a minister, doesn't care for such things."

"Then I hope you'll let me see you home," said Ben gallantly.

"I wouldn't like to trouble you," said Rose, with a spice of coquetry. "It will take you out of your way."

"I don't mind that," said Ben eagerly.

"Besides there won't be any need. You say the tramp isn't in the village."

"On second thoughts, I think it very likely he is," said Ben.

"If you really think so - " commenced Rose, with cunning hesitation.

"I feel quite sure of it. He's a terrible looking fellow."

Rose smiled to herself. She meant all the time to accept Ben's escort, for he was a bright, attractive boy, and she liked his society.

"Then perhaps I had better accept your offer, but I am sorry to give you so much trouble."

"No trouble at all," said Ben promptly.

Just then Prof. Harrington came forward and made his introductory speech.

"For my first experiment, ladies and gentlemen," he said, when this was over, "I should like a pocket handkerchief."

A countrified-looking young man on the front seat, anxious to share in the glory of the coming trick, produced a flaming red bandanna from his pocket and tendered it with outstretched hand.

"You are very kind," said the professor, "but this will hardly answer my purpose. I should prefer a linen handkerchief. Will some young lady oblige me?"

"Let him have yours, Rose," suggested Ben.

Rose had no objection, and it was passed to the professor.

"The young lady will give me leave to do what I please with the handkerchief?" asked the professor.

Rose nodded assent.

"Then," said the professor, "I will see if it is proof against fire."

He deliberately unfolded it, crushed it in his hand, and then held it in the flame of a candle.

Rose uttered a low ejaculation.

"That's the last of your handkerchief, Rose," said Ben.

"You made me give it to him. You must buy me another," said the young lady.

"So I will, if you don't get it back safe."

"How can I?"

"I don't know. Perhaps the professor does," answered Ben.

"Really," said the professor, contemplating the handkerchief regretfully. "I am afraid I have destroyed the handkerchief; I hope the young lady will pardon me."

He looked at Rose, but she made no sign. She felt a little disturbed, for it was a fine handkerchief, given her by her aunt.

"I see the young lady is annoyed," continued the magician. "In that case I must try to repair damages. I made a little mistake in supposing the handkerchief to be noncombustible. However, perhaps matters are not so bad as they seem."

He tossed the handkerchief behind a screen, and moved forward to a table on which was a neat box. Taking a small key from his pocket, he unlocked it and drew forth before the astonished eyes of his audience the handkerchief intact.

"I believe this is your handkerchief, is it not?" he asked, stepping down from the platform and handing it back to Rose.

"Yes," answered Rose, in amazement, examining it carefully, and unable to detect any injury.

"And it is in as good condition as when you gave it to me?"

"Yes, sir."

"So much the better. Then I shall not be at the expense of buying a new one. Young man, have you any objections to lending me your hat?"

This question was addressed to Ben.

"No, sir."

"Thank you. I will promise not to burn it, as I did the young lady's handkerchief. You are sure there is nothing in it?"

"Yes, sir."

By this time the magician had reached the platform.

"I am sorry to doubt the young gentleman's word," said the professor, "but I will charitably believe he is mistaken. Perhaps he forgot these articles when he said it was empty," and he drew forth a couple of potatoes and half a dozen onions from the hat and laid them on the table.

There was a roar of laughter from the audience, and Ben looked rather confused, especially when Rose turned to him and, laughing, said:

"You've been robbing Mr. Crawford, I am

afraid, Ben."

"The young gentleman evidently uses his hat for a market-basket," proceeded the professor. "Rather a strange taste, but this is a free country. But what have we here?"

Out came a pair of stockings, a napkin and a necktie.

"Very convenient to carry your wardrobe about with you," said the professor, "though it is rather curious taste to put them with vegetables. But here is something else," and the magician produced a small kitten, who regarded the audience with startled eyes and uttered a timid moan.

"Oh, Ben! let me have that pretty kitten," said Rose.

"It's none of mine!" said Ben, half annoyed, half amused.

"I believe there is nothing more," said the professor.

He carried back the hat to Ben, and gave it to him with the remark:

"Young man, you may call for your vegetables and other articles after the entertainment."

"You are welcome to them," said Ben.

"Thank you; you are very liberal."

When at length the performance was over, Ben and Rose moved toward the door. As Rose reached the outer door, a boy about Ben's age, but considerably better dressed, stepped up to her and said, with a consequential air:

"I will see you home, Miss Gardiner."

"Much obliged, Mr. Davenport," said Rose, "but I have accepted Ben's escort."

CHAPTER VI

TWO YOUNG RIVALS

Tom Davenport, for it was the son of Squire Davenport who had offered his escort to Rose, glanced superciliously at our hero.

"I congratulate you on having secured a grocer's boy as escort," he said in a tone of annoyance.

Ben's fist contracted, and he longed to give the pretentious aristocrat a lesson, but he had the good sense to wait for the young lady's reply.

"I accept your congratulations, Mr. Davenport," said Rose coldly. "I have no desire to change my escort."

Tom Davenport laughed derisively, and walked away.

"I'd like to box his ears," said Ben, reddening.

"He doesn't deserve your notice, Ben," said Rose, taking his arm.

But Ben was not easily appeased.

"Just because his father is a rich man," he resumed.

"He presumes upon it," interrupted Rose, good-naturedly. "Well, let him. That's his chief claim to consideration, and it is natural for him to make the most of it."

"At any rate, I hope that can't be said of me," returned Ben, his brow clearing. "If I had nothing but money to be proud of, I should be very poorly off."

"You wouldn't object to it, though."

"No, I hope, for mother's sake, some day to be rich."

"Most of our rich men were once poor boys," said Rose quietly. "I have a book of biographies at home, and I find that not only rich men, but men distinguished in other ways, generally commenced in poverty."

"I wish you'd lend me that book," said Ben. "Sometimes I get despondent and that will give me courage."

"You shall have it whenever you call at the house. But you mustn't think too much of getting money."

"I don't mean to; but I should like to make my mother comfortable. I don't see much chance of it while I remain a 'grocer's boy,' as Tom Davenport calls me."

"Better be a grocer's boy than spend your time in idleness, as Tom does."

"Tom thinks it beneath him to work."

"If his father had been of the sane mind when he was a

boy, he would never have become a rich man."

"Was Squire Davenport a poor boy?"

"Yes, so uncle told me the other day. When he was a boy he worked on a farm. I don't know how he made his money, but I presume he laid the foundation of his wealth by hard work. So, Tom hasn't any right to look down upon those who are beginning now as his father began."

They had by this time traversed half the distance from the Town Hall to the young lady's home. The subject of conversation was changed and they began to talk about the evening's entertainment. At length they reached the minister's house.

"Won't you come in, Ben?" asked Rose.

"Isn't it too late?"

"No, uncle always sits up late reading, and will be glad to see you."

"Then I will come in for a few minutes."

Ben's few minutes extended to three-quarters of an hour. When he came out, the moon was obscured and it was quite dark. Ben had not gone far when he heard steps behind him, and presently a hand was laid on his shoulder.

"Hello, boy!" said a rough voice.

Ben started, and turning suddenly, recognized in spite of the darkness, the tramp who had attempted to rob

Horatio Alger, Jr.

him during the day. He paused, uncertain whether he was not going to be attacked, but the tramp laughed reassuringly.

"Don't be afraid, boy," he said. "I owe you some money, and here it is."

He pressed into the hand of the astonished Ben the dollar which our hero had given him.

"I don't think it will do me any good," he said. "I've given it back, and now you can't say I robbed you."

"You are a strange man," said Ben.

"I'm not so bad as I look," said the tramp. "Some day I may do you a service. I'm goin' out of town to-night, and you'll hear from me again some time."

He turned swiftly, and Ben lost sight of him.

CHAPTER VII

THE TRAMP MAKES ANOTHER CALL

My readers will naturally be surprised at the tramp's restitution of a coin, which, though counterfeit, he would probably have managed to pass, but this chapter will throw some light on his mysterious conduct.

When he made a sudden exit from Mrs. Barclay's house, upon the appearance of the squire and his friend, he did not leave the premises, but posted himself at a window, slightly open, of the room in which the widow received her new visitors. He listened with a smile to the squire's attempt to force Mrs. Barclay to sell her house.

"He's a sly old rascal!" thought the tramp. "I'll put a spoke in his wheel."

When the squire and his wife's cousin left the house, the tramp followed at a little distance. Not far from the squire's handsome residence Kirk left him, and the tramp then came boldly forward.

"Good-evenin'," he said familiarly.

Squire Davenport turned sharply, and as his eye fell on the unprepossessing figure, he instinctively put his

Horatio Alger, Jr.

hand in the pocket in which he kept his wallet.

"Who are you?" he demanded apprehensively.

"I ain't a thief, and you needn't fear for your wallet," was the reply.

"Let me pass, fellow! I can do nothing for you."

"We'll see about that!"

"Do you threaten me?" asked Squire Davenport, in alarm.

"Not at all; but I've got some business with you - some important business."

"Then call to-morrow forenoon," said Davenport, anxious to get rid of his ill-looking acquaintance.

"That won't do; I want to leave town tonight."

"That's nothing to me."

"It may be," said the tramp significantly. "I want to speak to you about the husband of the woman you called on to-night."

"The husband of Mrs. Barclay! Why, he is dead!" ejaculated the squire, in surprise.

"That is true. Do you know whether he left any property?"

"No, I believe not."

"That's what I want to talk about. You'd better see me to-night."

There was significance in the tone of the tramp, and Squire Davenport looked at him searchingly.

"Why don't you go and see Mrs. Barclay about this matter?" he asked.

"I may, but I think you'd better see me first."

By this time they had reached the Squire's gate.

"Come in," he said briefly.

The squire led the way into a comfortable sitting room, and his rough visitor followed him. By the light of an astral lamp Squire Davenport looked at him.

"Did I ever see you before?" he asked.

"Probably not."

"Then I don't see what business we can have together. I am tired, and wish to go to bed."

"I'll come to business at once, then. When John Barclay died in Chicago, a wallet was found in his pocket, and in that wallet was a promissory note for a thousand dollars, signed by you. I suppose you have paid that sum to the widow?"

Squire Davenport was the picture of dismay. He had meanly ignored the note, with the intention of cheating Mrs. Barclay. He had supposed it was lost, yet here, after some years, appeared a man who knew of it. As

Mr. Barclay had been reticent about his business affairs, he had never told his wife about having deposited this sum with Squire Davenport, and of this fact the squire had meanly taken advantage.

"What proof have you of this strange and improbable story?" asked the squire, after a nervous pause.

"The best of proof," answered the tramp promptly. "The note was found and is now in existence."

"Who holds it - that is, admitting for a moment the truth of your story?"

"I do; it is in my pocket at this moment."

At this moment Tom Davenport opened the door of the apartment, and stared in open-eyed amazement at his father's singular visitor.

"Leave the room, Tom," said his father hastily. "This man is consulting me on business."

"Is that your son, squire?" asked the tramp, with a familiar nod. "He's quite a young swell."

"What business can my father have with such a cad?" thought Tom, disgusted.

Tom was pleased, nevertheless, at being taken for "a young swell."

CHAPTER VIII

SQUIRE DAVENPORT'S FINANCIAL OPERATION

Squire Davenport was a thoroughly respectable man in the estimation of the community. That such a man was capable of defrauding a poor widow, counting on her ignorance, would have plunged all his friends and acquaintances into the profoundest amazement.

Yet this was precisely what the squire had done.

Mr. Barclay, who had prospered beyond his wife's knowledge, found himself seven years before in possession of a thousand dollars in hard cash. Knowing that the squire had a better knowledge of suitable investments than he, he went to him one day and asked advice. Now, the squire was fond of money. When he saw the ample roll of bank notes which his neighbor took from his wallet, he felt a desire to possess them. They would not be his, to be sure, but merely to have them under his control seemed pleasant. So he said:

"Friend Barclay, I should need time to consider that question. Are you in a hurry?"

"I should like to get the money out of my possession. I might lose it or have it stolen. Besides, I don't want my wife to discover that I have it."

"It might make her extravagant, perhaps," suggested the squire.

"No, I am not afraid of that; but I want some day to surprise her by letting her see that I am a richer man than she thinks."

"Very judicious! Then no one knows that you have the money?"

"No one; I keep my business to myself."

"You are a wise man. I'll tell you what I will do, friend Barclay. While I am not prepared to recommend any particular investment, I will take the money and give you my note for it, agreeing to pay six per cent. interest. Of course I shall invest it in some way, and I may gain or I may lose, but even if I do lose you will be safe, for you will have my note, and will receive interest semi-annually."

The proposal struck Mr. Barclay quite favorably.

"I suppose I can have the money when I want it again?" he inquired.

"Oh, certainly! I may require a month's notice to realize on securities; but if I have the money in bank I won't even ask that."

"Then take the money, squire, and give me the note."

So, in less than five minutes, the money found its way into Squire Davenport's strong box, and Mr. Barclay left the squire's presence well satisfied with his note of hand in place of his roll of greenbacks.

Nearly two years passed. Interest was paid punctually three times, and another payment was all but due when the unfortunate creditor died in Chicago. Then it was that a terrible temptation assailed Squire Davenport. No one knew of the trust his neighbor had reposed in him - not even his wife. Of course, if the note was found in his pocket, all would be known. But perhaps it would not be known. In that case, the thousand dollars and thirty dollars interest might be retained without anyone being the wiser.

It is only fair to say that Squire Davenport's face flushed with shame as the unworthy thought came to him, but still he did not banish it. He thought the matter over, and the more he thought the more unwilling he was to give up this sum, which all at once had become dearer to him than all the rest of his possessions.

"I'll wait to see whether the note is found," he said to himself. "Of course, if it is, I will pay it - " That is, he would pay it if he were obliged to do it.

Poor Barclay was buried in Chicago - it would have been too expensive to bring on the body - and pretty soon it transpired that he had left no property, except the modest cottage in which his widow and son continued to live.

Poor Mrs. Barclay! Everybody pitied her, and lamented her straitened circumstances. Squire Davenport kept silence, and thought, with guilty joy, "They haven't found the note; I can keep the money, and no

Horatio Alger, Jr.

one will be the wiser!"

How a rich man could have been guilty of such consummate meaness I will not undertake to explain, but "the love of money is the root of evil," and Squire Davenport had love of money in no common measure.

Five years passed. Mrs. Barclay was obliged to mortgage her house to obtain the means of living, and the very man who supplied her with the money was the very man whom her husband had blindly trusted. She little dreamed that it was her own money he was doling out to her.

In fact, Squire Davenport himself had almost forgotten it. He had come to consider the thousand dollars and interest fully and absolutely his own, and had no apprehension that his mean fraud would ever be discovered. Like a thunderbolt, then, came to him the declaration of his unsavory visitor that the note was in existence, and was in the hands of a man who meant to use it. Smitten with sudden panic, he stared in the face of the tramp. But he was not going to give up without a struggle.

"You are evidently trying to impose upon me," he said, mentally bracing up. "You wish to extort money from me."

"So I do," said the tramp quietly.

"Ha! you admit it?" exclaimed the squire.

"Certainly; I wouldn't have taken the trouble to come here at great expense and inconvenience if I hadn't been expecting to make some money."

"Then you have come to the wrong person; I repeat it, you've come to the wrong person!" said the squire, straightening his back and eying his companion sternly.

"I begin to think I have," assented the visitor.

"Ha! he weakens!" thought Squire Davenport. "My good man, I recommend you to turn over a new leaf, and seek to earn an honest living, instead of trying to levy blackmail on men of means."

"An honest living!" repeated the tramp, with a laugh. "This advice comes well from you."

Once more the squire felt uncomfortable and apprehensive.

"I don't understand you," he said irritably. "However, as you yourself admit, you have come to the wrong person."

"Just so," said the visitor, rising. "I now go to the right person."

"What do you mean?" asked Squire Davenport, in alarm.

"I mean that I ought to have gone to Mrs. Barclay."

"Sit down, sit down!" said the squire nervously. "You mustn't do that."

"Why not?" demanded the tramp, looking him calmly in the face.

"Because it would disturb her mind, and excite erroneous thoughts and expectations."

"She would probably be willing to give me a good sum for bringing it to her, say, the overdue interest. That alone, in five years and a half, would amount to over three hundred dollars, even without compounding."

Squire Davenport groaned in spirit. It was indeed true! He must pay away over thirteen hundred dollars, and his loss in reputation would be even greater than his loss of money.

"Can't we compromise this thing?" he stammered. "I don't admit the genuineness of the note, but if such a claim were made, it would seriously annoy me. I am willing to give you, say, fifty dollars, if you will deliver up the pretended note."

"It won't do, squire. Fifty dollars won't do! I won't take a cent less than two hundred, and that is only about half the interest you would have to pay."

"You speak as if the note were genuine," said the squire uncomfortably.

"You know whether it is or not," said the tramp significantly. "At any rate, we won't talk about that. You know my terms."

In the end Squire Davenport paid over two hundred dollars, and received back the note, which after a hasty examination, he threw into the fire.

"Now," he said roughly, "get out of my house, you - forger."

"Good-evening, squire," said the tramp, laughing and nodding to the discomfited squire. "We may meet again, some time."

"If you come here again, I will set the dog on you."

"So much the worse for the dog! Well, good-night! I have enjoyed my interview - hope you have."

"Impudent scoundrel!" said the squire to himself. "I hope he will swing some day!"

But, as he thought over what had happened, he found comfort in the thought that the secret was at last safe. The note was burned, and could never reappear in judgment against him. Certainly, he got off cheap.

"Well," thought the tramp as he strode away from the squire's mansion, "this has been a profitable evening. I have two hundred dollars in my pocket, and - I still have a hold on the rascal. If he had only examined the note before burning it, he might have made a discovery!"

CHAPTER IX

A PROSPECT OF TROUBLE

When Ben returned home from the Town Hall he discovered, at the first glance, that his mother was in trouble.

"Are you disturbed because I came home so late?" asked Ben. "I would have been here sooner, but I went home with Rose Gardiner. I ought to have remembered that you might feel lonely."

Mrs. Barclay smiled faintly.

"I had no occasion to feel lonely," she said. "I had three callers. The last did not go away till after nine o'clock."

"I am glad you were not alone, mother," said Ben, thinking some of his mother's neighbors might have called.

"I should rather have been alone, Ben. They brought bad news - that is, one of them did."

"Who was it, mother? Who called on you?"

"The first one was the same man who took your money

in the woods."

"What, the tramp!" exclaimed Ben hastily. "Did he frighten you?"

"A little, at first, but he did me no harm. He asked for some supper, and I gave it to him."

"What bad news did he bring?"

"None. It was not he. On the other hand, what he hinted would be good news if it were true. He said that your father left property, and that he was the only man that possessed the secret."

"Do you think this can be so?" said Ben, looking at his mother in surprise.

"I don't know what to think. He said he was a barkeeper in the hotel where your poor father died, and was about to say more when a knock was heard at the door, and he hurried away, as if in fear of encountering somebody."

"And he did not come back?"

"No."

"That is strange," said Ben thoughtfully. "Do you know, mother, I met him on my way home, or rather, he came up behind me and tapped me on the shoulder."

"What did be say?" asked Mrs. Barclay eagerly.

"He gave me back the bogus dollar he took from me saying, with a laugh, that it would be of no use to him.

Then he said he might do me a service sometime, and I would some day hear from him."

"Ben, I think that man took the papers from the pocket of your dying father, and has them now in his possession. He promised to sell me a secret for money, but I told him I had none to give."

"I wish we could see him again, but he said he should leave town to-night. But, mother, what was the bad news you spoke of?"

"Ben, I am afraid we are going to lose our home," said the widow, the look of trouble returning to her face.

"What do you mean, mother?"

"You know that Squire Davenport has a mortgage on the place for seven hundred dollars; he was here to-night with a man named Kirk, some connection of his wife. It seems Kirk is coming to Pentonville to live, and wants this house."

"He will have to want it, mother," said Ben stoutly.

"Not if the squire backs him as he does; he threatens to foreclose the mortgage if I don't sell."

Ben comprehended the situation now, and appreciated its gravity.

"What does he offer, Mother?"

"A thousand dollars only - perhaps a little more."

"Why that would be downright robbery."

"Not in the eye of the law. Ben, we are in the power of Squire Davenport, and he is a hard man."

"I would like to give him a piece of my mind, mother. He might be in better business than robbing you of your house."

"Do nothing hastily, Ben. There is only one thing that we can do to save the house, and that is, to induce someone to advance the money necessary to take up the mortgage."

"Can you think of anybody who would do it?"

Mrs. Barclay shook her head.

"There is no one in Pentonville who would be willing, and has the money," she said. "I have a rich cousin in New York, but I have not met him since I was married; he thought a great deal of me once, but I suppose he scarcely remembers me now. He lived, when I last heard of him, on Lexington Avenue, and his name is Absalom Peters."

"And he is rich?"

"Yes, very rich, I believe."

"I have a great mind to ask for a day's vacation from Mr. Crawford, and go to New York to see him."

"I am afraid it would do no good."

"It would do no harm, except that it would cost something for traveling expenses. But I would go as economically as possible. Have I your permission, mother?"

"You can do as you like, Ben; I won't forbid you, though I have little hope of its doing any good."

"Then I will try and get away Monday. To-morrow is Saturday, and I can't be spared at the store; there is always more doing, you know, on Saturday than any other day."

"I don't feel like giving any advice, Ben. Do as you please."

The next day, on his way home to dinner, Ben met his young rival of the evening previous, Tom Davenport.

"How are you, Tom?" said Ben, nodding.

"I want to speak to you, Ben Barclay," said the young aristocrat, pausing in his walk.

"Go ahead! I'm listening," said Ben.

Tom was rather annoyed at the want of respect which, in his opinion, Ben showed him, but hardly knew how to express his objections, so he came at once to the business in hand.

"You'd better not hang around Rose Gardiner so much," he said superciliously.

"What do you mean by that?" demanded Ben quickly.

"You forced your attentions on her last evening at the Town Hall."

"Who told you so?"

"I saw it for myself."

"I thought Rose didn't tell you so."

"It must be disagreeable to her family to have a common grocer's boy seen with her."

"It seems to me you take a great deal of interest in the matter, Tom Davenport. You talk as if you were the guardian of the young lady. I believe you wanted to go home with her yourself."

"It would have been far more suitable, but you had made her promise to go with you."

"I would have released her from her promise at once, if she had expressed a wish to that effect. Now, I want to give you a piece of advice."

"I don't want any of your advice," said Tom loftily. "I don't want any advice from a store boy."

"I'll give it to you all the same. You can make money by minding your own business."

"You are impudent!" said Tom, flushing with anger. "I've got something more to tell you. You'll be out on the sidewalk before three months are over. Father is going to foreclose the mortgage on your house."

"That remains to be seen!" said Ben, but his heart sank within him as he realized that the words would probably prove true.

CHAPTER X

BEN GOES TO NEW YORK

Pentonville was thirty-five miles distant from New York, and the fare was a dollar, but an excursion ticket, carrying a passenger both ways, was only a dollar and a half. Ben calculated that his extra expenses, including dinner, might amount to fifty cents, thus making the cost of the trip two dollars. This sum, small as it was, appeared large both to Ben and his mother. Some doubts about the expediency of the journey suggested themselves to Mrs. Barclay.

"Do you think you had better go, Ben?" she said doubtfully. "Two dollars would buy you some new stockings and handkerchiefs."

"I will do without them, mother. Something has got to be done, or we shall be turned into the street when three months are up. Squire Davenport is a very selfish man, and he will care nothing for our comfort or convenience."

"That is true," said the widow, with a sigh. "If I thought your going to New York would do any good, I would not grudge you the money - "

"Something will turn up, or I will turn up something,"

said Ben confidently.

When he asked Mr. Crawford for a day off, the latter responded: "Yes, Ben, I think I can spare you, as Monday is not a very busy day. Would you be willing to do an errand for me?"

"Certainly Mr. Crawford, with pleasure."

"I need a new supply of prints. Go to Stackpole & Rogers, No. - White Street, and select me some attractive patterns. I shall rely upon your taste."

"Thank you, sir," said Ben, gratified by the compliment.

He received instructions as to price and quantity, which he carefully noted down.

"As it will save me a journey, not to speak of my time, I am willing to pay your fare one way."

"Thank you, sir; you are very kind."

Mr. Crawford took from the money drawer a dollar, and handed it to Ben.

"But I buy an excursion ticket, so that my fare each way will be but seventy-five cents."

"Never mind, the balance will go toward your dinner."

"There, mother, what do you say now?" said Ben, on Saturday night. "Mr. Crawford is going to pay half my expenses, and I am going to buy some goods for him."

"I am glad he reposes so much confidence in you, Ben. I hope you won't lose his money."

"Oh, I don't carry any. He buys on thirty days. All I have to do is to select the goods."

"Perhaps it is for the best that you go, after all," said Mrs. Barclay. "At any rate, I hope so."

At half-past seven o'clock on Monday morning Ben stood on the platform of the Pentonville station, awaiting the arrival of the train.

"Where are you going?" said a voice.

Ben, turning, saw that it was Tom Davenport who had spoken.

"I am going to New York," he answered briefly.

"Has Crawford discharged you?"

"Why do you ask? Would you like to apply for the position?" asked Ben coolly.

"Do you think I would condescend to be a grocer's boy?" returned Tom disdainfully.

"I don't know."

"If I go into business it will be as a merchant."

"I am glad to hear it."

"You didn't say what you were going to New York for?"

"I have no objection to tell you, as you are anxious to know; I am going to the city to buy goods."

Tom looked not only amazed, but incredulous.

"That's a likely story," said he, after a pause.

"It is a true story."

"Do you mean to say Crawford trusts you buy goods for him?"

"So it seems."

"He must be getting weak-headed."

"Suppose you call and give him that gratifying piece of information."

Just then the train came thundering up, and Ben jumped aboard. Tom Davenport looked after him with a puzzled glance.

"I wonder whether that boy tells the truth," he said to himself. "He thinks too much of himself, considering what he is."

It never occurred to Tom that the remark would apply even better to him than the boy he was criticising. As a rule we are the last to recognize our own faults, however quick we may be to see the faults of others.

Two hours later Ben stood in front of the large dry-goods jobbing house of Stackpole & Rogers, in White Street.

He ascended the staircase to the second floor, which was very spacious and filled with goods in great variety.

"Where is the department of prints?" he inquired of a young man near the door.

He was speedily directed and went over at once. He showed the salesman in charge a letter from Mr. Crawford, authorizing him to select a certain amount of goods.

"You are rather a young buyer," said the salesman, smiling.

"It is the first time I have served in that way," said Ben modestly; "but I know pretty well what Mr. Crawford wants."

Half an hour was consumed in making his selections.

"You have good taste," said the salesman, "judging from your selections."

"Thank you."

"If you ever come to the city to look for work, come here, and I will introduce you to the firm."

"Thank you. How soon can you ship the goods?"

"I am afraid not to-day, as we are very busy. Early next week we will send them."

His business concluded, Ben left the store and walked up to Broadway. The crowded thoroughfare had much to interest him. He was looking at a window when someone tapped him on the shoulder.

It was a young man foppishly attired, who was smiling graciously upon him.

"Why, Gus Andre," he said, "when did you come to town, and how did you leave all the folks in Bridgeport?"

"You have made a mistake," said Ben.

"Isn't your name Gus Andre?"

"No, it is Ben Barclay, from Pentonville."

"I really beg your pardon. You look surprisingly like my friend Gussie."

Five minutes later there was another tap on our hero's shoulder, as he was looking into another window, and another nicely dressed young man said heartily: "Why, Ben, my boy, when did you come to town?"

"This morning," answered Ben. "You seem to know me, but I can't remember you."

"Are you not Ben Barclay, of Pentonville."

"Yes, but - "

"Don't you remember Jim Fisher, who passed part of the summer, two years since, in your village?"

"Where were you staying?" asked Ben.

It was the other's turn to looked confused.

"At - the Smiths'," he answered, at random.

"At Mrs. Roxana Smith's?" suggested Ben.

"Yes, yes," said the other eagerly, "she is my aunt."

"Is she?" asked Ben, with a smile of amusement, for he had by this time made up his mind as to the character of his new friend. "She must be proud of her stylish nephew. Mrs. Smith is a poor widow, and takes in washing."

"It's some other Smith," said the young man, discomfited.

"She is the only one by that name in Pentonville."

Jim Fisher, as he called himself, turned upon his heel and left Ben without a word. It was clear that nothing could be made out of him.

Ben walked all the way up Broadway, as far as Twenty-first Street, into which he turned, and walked eastward until he reached Gramercy Park, opposite which Lexington Avenue starts. In due time he reached the house of Mr. Absalom Peters, and, ascending the steps, he rang the bell.

"Is Mr. Peters in?" he asked of the servant who answered the bell.

"No."

"Will he be in soon?"

"I guess not. He sailed for Europe last week."

Ben's heart sank within him. He had hoped much from Mr. Peters, before whom he meant to lay all the facts of his mother's situation. Now that hope was crushed.

He turned and slowly descended the steps.

"There goes our last chance of saving the house," he said to himself sadly.

CHAPTER XI

THE MADISON AVENUE STAGE

Ben was naturally hopeful, but he had counted more than he was aware on the chance of obtaining assistance from Absalom Peters toward paying off his mother's mortgage. As Mr. Peters was in Europe nothing could be done, and them seemed absolutely no one else to apply to. They had friends, of course, and warm ones, in Pentonville, but none that were able to help them.

"I suppose we must make up our minds to lose the house," thought Ben. "Squire Davenport is selfish and grasping, and there is little chance of turning him."

He walked westward till he reached Madison Avenue. A stage approached, being bound downtown, and, feeling tired, he got in. The fare was but five cents, and he was willing to pay it.

Some half dozen other passengers beside himself were in the stage. Opposite Ben sat a handsomely dressed, somewhat portly lady, of middle age, with a kindly expression. Next her sat a young man, attired fashionably, who had the appearance of belonging to a family of position. There were, besides, an elderly man, of clerical appearance; a nurse with a small child, a business man, intent upon the financial column of a leading paper, and a schoolboy.

Ben regarded his fellow-passengers with interest. In Pentonville he seldom saw a new face. Here all were new. Our young hero was, though be did not know it, an embryo student of human nature. He liked to observe men and women of different classes and speculate upon their probable position and traits. It so happened that his special attention was attracted to the fashionably-attired young man.

"I suppose he belongs to a rich family, and has plenty of money," thought Ben. "It must be pleasant to be born with a gold spoon in your mouth, and know that you are provided for life."

If Ben had been wiser he would have judged differently. To be born to wealth removes all the incentives to action, and checks the spirit of enterprise. A boy or man who finds himself gradually rising in the world, through his own exertions, experiences a satisfaction unknown to one whose fortune is ready-made. However, in Ben's present strait it is no wonder he regarded with envy the supposed young man of fortune.

Our hero was destined to be strangely surprised. His eyes were unusually keen, and enabled him after a while to observe some rather remarkable movements on the part of the young man. Though his eyes were looking elsewhere, Ben could see that his right hand was stealthily insinuating itself into the pocket of the richly-dressed lady at his side.

"Is it possible that he is a pickpocket?" thought Ben, in

amazement. "So nicely dressed as he is, too!"

It did not occur to Ben that he dressed well the better to avert suspicion from his real character. Besides, a man who lives at other people's expense can afford to dress well.

"What shall I do?" thought Ben, disturbed in mind. "Ought I not to warn the lady that she is in danger of losing her money?"

While he was hesitating the deed was accomplished. A pearl portemonnaie was adroitly drawn from the lady's pocket and transferred to that of the young man. It was done with incredible swiftness, but Ben's sharp eyes saw it.

The young man yawned, and, turning away from the lady, appeared to be looking out of a window at the head of the coach.

"Why, there is Jack Osborne," he said, half audibly, and, rising, pulled the strap for the driver to stop the stage.

Then was the critical moment for Ben. Was he to allow the thief to escape with the money. Ben hated to get into a disturbance, but he felt that it would be wrong and cowardly to be silent.

"Before you get out," he said, "hand that lady her pocketbook."

The face of the pickpocket changed and he darted a malignant glance at Ben.

"What do you mean, you young scoundrel?" he said.

"You have taken that lady's pocketbook," persisted Ben.

"Do you mean to insult me?"

"I saw you do it."

With a half exclamation of anger, the young man darted to the door. But he was brought to a standstill by the business man, who placed himself in his way.

"Not so fast, young man," he said resolutely.

"Out of the way!" exclaimed the thief, in a rage. "It's all a base lie. I never was so insulted in my life."

"Do you miss your pocketbook, madam?" asked the gentleman, turning to the lady who had been robbed.

"Yes," she answered. "It was in the pocket next to this man."

The thief seeing there was no hope of retaining his booty, drew it from his pocket and flung it into the lady's lap.

"Now, may I go?" he said.

There was no policeman in sight, and at a nod from the lady, the pickpocket was allowed to leave the stage.

"You ought to have had him arrested. He is a dangerous character," said the gentleman who had barred his progress.

Horatio Alger, Jr.

"It would have been inconvenient for me to appear against him," said the lady. "I am willing to let him go."

"Well, there is one comfort - if he keeps on he will be hauled up sooner or later," remarked the gentleman. "Would your loss have been a heavy one?" he inquired.

"I had quite a large sum in my pocketbook, over two hundred dollars. But for my young friend opposite," she said, nodding kindly at Ben, "I should have lost it with very small chance of recovery."

"I am glad to have done you a service, madam," said Ben politely.

"I know it is rather imprudent to carry so large sum about with me," continued the lady, but I have a payment to make to a carpenter who has done work in my house, and I thought he might not find it convenient use a check."

"A lady is in more danger than a gentleman," observed the business man, "as she cannot so well hide away her pocketbook. You will need to be careful as you walk along the street."

"I think it will be best to have a neighbor whom I can trust," said the lady. "Would you mind taking this seat at my side?" she continued, addressing Ben.

"I will change with pleasure," said our hero, taking the seat recently vacated by the pickpocket.

"You have sharp eyes, my young friend," said his new acquaintance.

"My eyes are pretty good," said Ben, with a smile.

"They have done me good service to-day. May I know to whom I am indebted for such timely help?"

"My name is Benjamin Barclay."

"Do you live in the city?"

"No, madam. I live in Pentonville, about thirty miles from New York."

"I have heard of the place. Are you proposing to live here?"

"No madam. I came in to-day on a little business of my own, and also to select some goods for a country store in which I am employed."

"You are rather young for such a commission."

"I know the sort of goods Mr. Crawford sells, so it was not very difficult to make the selection."

"At what time do you go back?"

"By the four o'clock train."

"Have you anything to do meanwhile?"

"No, madam," answered Ben, a little surprised.

"Then I should like to have you accompany me to the place where I am to settle my bill. I feel rather timid after my adventure with our late fellow-passenger."

"I shall be very happy to oblige you, madam," said Ben politely.

He had just heard a public clock strike one and he knew, therefore, that he would have plenty of time.

CHAPTER XII

BEN'S LUCK

"We will get out here," said Mrs. Hamilton.

They had reached the corner of Fourth Street and Broadway.

Ben pulled the strap, and with his new friend left the stage. He offered his hand politely to assist the lady in descending.

"He is a little gentleman," thought Mrs. Hamilton, who was much pleased with our hero.

They turned from Broadway eastward, and presently crossed the Bowery also. Not far to the east of the last avenue they came to a carpenter's shop.

Mr. Plank, a middle-aged, honest-looking mechanic, looked up in surprise when Mrs. Hamilton entered the shop.

"You didn't expect a call from me?" said the lady pleasantly.

"No, ma'am. Fashionable ladies don't often find their way over here."

"Then don't look upon me as a fashionable lady. I like to attend to my business myself, and have brought you the money for your bill."

"Thank you, ma'am. You never made me wait. But I am sorry you had the trouble to come to my shop. I would have called at your house if you had sent me a postal."

"My time was not so valuable as yours, Mr. Plank. I must tell you, however, that you came near not getting your money this morning. Another person undertook to collect your bill."

"Who was it?" demanded the carpenter indignantly. "If there's anybody playing such tricks on me I will have him up before the courts."

"It was no acquaintance of yours. The person in question had no spite against you and you would only have suffered a little delay."

Then Mrs. Hamilton explained how a pickpocket had undertaken to relieve her of her wallet, and would have succeeded but for her young companion.

"Oh they're mighty sharp, ma'am, I can tell you," said the carpenter. "I never lost anything, because I don't look as if I had anything worth stealing; but if one of those rascals made up his mind to rob me, ten to one he'd do it."

Mr. Plank receipted his bill and Mrs. Hamilton paid him a hundred and eighty-seven dollars and fifty cents. Ben could not help envying him as he saw the roll of bills transferred to him.

"I hope the work was done satisfactory," said Mr. Plank. (Perfect grammar could not be expected of a man who, from the age of twelve, had been forced to earn his own living.)

"Quite so, Mr. Plank," said the lady graciously. "I shall send for you when I have any more work to be done."

There was no more business to attend to, and Mrs. Hamilton led the way out, accompanied by Ben.

"I will trouble you to see me as far as Broadway," said the lady. "I am not used to this neighborhood and prefer to have an escort."

"I didn't think this morning," said Ben to himself, "that a rich lady would select me as her escort."

On the whole, he liked it. It gave him a feeling of importance, and a sense of responsibility which a manly boy always likes.

"I shall be glad to stay with you as long as you like," said Ben.

"Thank you, Benjamin, or shall I say Ben?"

"I wish you would. I hardly know myself when I am called Benjamin."

"As we are walking alone, suppose you tell me something of yourself. I only know your name, and that you live in Pentonville. What relations have you?"

"A mother only - my father is dead."

"And you help take care of your mother, I suppose?"

"Yes; father left us nothing except the house we live in, or, at least, we could get track of no other property. He died in Chicago suddenly."

"I hope you are getting along comfortably - you and your mother," said Mrs. Hamilton kindly.

"We have our troubles," answered Ben. "We are in danger of having our house taken from us."

"How is that?"

"A rich man in our village, Squire Davenport, has a mortgage of seven hundred dollars upon it. He wants the house for a relative of his wife, and threatens to foreclose at the end of three months."

"The house must be worth a good deal more than the mortgage."

"It is worth twice as much; but if it is put up at auction I doubt if it will fetch over a thousand dollars."

"This would leave your mother but three hundred?"

"Yes," answered Ben despondingly.

"Have you thought of any way of raising the money?"

"Yes; I came up to the city to-day to see a cousin of mother's, a Mr. Absalom Peters, who lives on Lexington Avenue, and I had just come from there when I got into the stage with you."

"Won't he help you?"

"Perhaps he might if he was in the city; though mother has seen nothing of him for twenty years; but, unfortunately, he just sailed for Europe."

"That is indeed a pity. I suppose you haven't much hope now?"

"Unless Mr. Peters comes back. He is the only one we can think of to call upon."

"What sort of a man is this Squire Davenport?"

"He is a very selfish man, who thinks only of his own interests. We felt safe, because we did not suppose he would have any use for a small house like ours; but night before last he called on mother with the man he wants it for."

"He cannot foreclose just yet, can he?" asked Mrs. Hamilton.

"No; we have three months to look around."

"Three months is a long time," said the lady cheerfully. "A good deal can happen in three months. Do the best you can, and keep up hope."

"I shall try to do so."

"You have reason to do so. You may not save your house, but you have, probably, a good many years before you, and plenty of good fortune may be in store for you."

The cheerful tone in which the lady spoke some how made Ben hopeful and sanguine, at any rate, for the time being.

"In this country, the fact that you are a poor boy will not stand in the way of your success. The most eminent men of the day, in all branches of business, and in all professions, were once poor boys. I dare say, looking at me, you don't suppose I ever knew anything of poverty."

"No," said Ben.

"Yet I was the daughter of a bankrupt farmer, and my husband was clerk in a country store. I am not going to tell you how he came to the city and prospered, leaving me, at his death, rich beyond my needs. Yet that is his history and mine. Does it encourage you?

"Yes, it does," answered Ben earnestly.

"It is for that reason, perhaps, that I take an interest in country boys who are placed as my husband once was," continued Mrs. Hamilton. "But here we are at Broadway. It only remains to express my acknowledgment of your timely assistance."

"You are quite welcome," said Ben.

"I am sure of that, but I am none the less indebted. Do me the favor to accept this."

She opened her portemonnaie, and taking from it a banknote, handed it to Ben.

In surprise he looked at it, and saw that it was a

twenty-dollar bill.

"Did you know this was a twenty-dollar bill?" he asked in amazement.

"Certainly," answered the lady, with a smile. "It is less than ten per cent. of the amount I would have lost but for you. I hope it will be of service to you."

"I feel rich with it," answered Ben. "How can I thank you, Mrs. Hamilton?"

"Call on me at No. - Madison Avenue, and do it in person, when you next come to the city," said the lady, smiling. "Now, if you will kindly call that stage, I will bid you good-by - for the present."

Ben complied with her request, and joyfully resumed his walk down Broadway.

CHAPTER XIII

A STARTLING EVENT

Though Ben had failed in the main object of his expedition, he returned to Pentonville in excellent spirits. He felt that he had been a favorite of fortune, and with good reason. In one day he had acquired a sum equal to five weeks' wages. Added to the dollar Mr. Crawford had contributed toward his expenses, he had been paid twenty-one dollars, while he had spent a little less than two. It is not every country boy who goes up to the great city who returns with an equal harvest. If Squire Davenport had not threatened to foreclose the mortgage, he would have felt justified in buying a present for his mother. As it was, he feared they would have need of all the money that came in to meet contingencies.

The train reached Pentonville at five o'clock, and about the usual time Ben opened the gate and walked up to the front door of his modest home. He looked so bright and cheerful when he entered her presence that Mrs. Barclay thought be must have found and been kindly received by the cousin whom he had gone up to seek.

"Did you see Mr. Peters?" she asked anxiously.

"No, mother; he is in Europe."

A shadow came over the mother's face. It was like taking from her her last hope.

"I was afraid you would not be repaid for going up to the city," she said.

"I made a pretty good day's work of it, nevertheless, mother. What do you say to this?" and he opened his wallet and showed her a roll of bills.

"Is that Mr. Crawford's money?" she asked.

"No, mother, it is mine, or rather it is yours, for I give it to you."

"Did you find a pocketbook, Ben? If so, the owner may turn up."

"Mother, the money is mine, fairly mine, for it was given me in return for a service I rendered a lady in New York."

"What service could you have possibly rendered, Ben, that merited such liberal payment?" asked his mother in surprise.

Upon this Ben explained, and Mrs. Barclay listened to his story with wonder.

"So you see, mother, I did well to go to the city," said Ben, in conclusion.

"It has turned out so, and I am thankful for your good fortune. But I should have been better pleased if you had seen Mr. Peters and found him willing to help us about the mortgage."

"So would I, mother, but this money is worth having. When supper is over I will go to the store to help out Mr. Crawford and report my purchase of goods. You know the most of our trade is in the evening."

After Ben had gone Mrs. Barclay felt her spirits return as she thought of the large addition to their little stock of money.

"One piece of good fortune may be followed by another," she thought. "Mr. Peters may return from Europe in time to help us. At any rate, we have nearly three months to look about us, and God may send us help."

When the tea dishes were washed and put away Mrs. Barclay sat down to mend a pair of Ben's socks, for in that household it was necessary to make clothing last as long as possible, when she was aroused from her work by a ringing at the bell.

She opened the door to admit Squire Davenport.

"Good-evening," she said rather coldly, for she could not feel friendly to a man who was conspiring to deprive her of her modest home and turn her out upon the sidewalk.

"Good-evening, widow," said the squire.

"Will you walk in?" asked Mrs. Barclay, not over cordially.

"Thank you, I will step in for five minutes. I called to see if you had thought better of my proposal the other evening."

"Your proposal was to take my house from me," said Mrs. Barclay. "How can you suppose I would think better of that?"

"You forget that the house is more mine than yours already, Mrs. Barclay. The sum I have advanced on mortgage is two-thirds of the value of the property."

"I dispute that, sir."

"Let it pass," said the squire, with a wave of the hand. "Call it three-fifths, if you will. Even then the property is more mine than yours. Women don't understand business, or you would see matters in a different light."

"I am a woman, it is true, but I understand very well that you wish to take advantage of me," said the widow, not without excusable bitterness.

"My good lady, you forget that I am ready to cancel the mortgage and pay you three hundred and fifty dollars for the house. Now, three hundred and fifty dollars is a handsome sum - a very handsome sum. You could put it in the savings bank and it would yield you quite a comfortable income."

"Twenty dollars, more or less," said Mrs. Barclay. "Is that what you call a comfortable income? How long do you think it would keep us alive?"

"Added, of course, to your son's wages. Ben is now able to earn good wages."

"He earns four dollars a week, and that is our main dependence."

"I congratulate you. I didn't suppose Mr. Crawford paid such high wages."

"Ben earns every cent of it."

"Very possibly. By the way, what is this that Tom was telling me about Ben being sent to New York to buy goods for the store?"

"It is true, if that is what you mean."

"Bless my soul! It is very strange of Crawford, and I may add, not very judicious."

"I suppose Mr. Crawford is the best judge of that, sir."

"Even if the boy were competent, which is not for a moment to be thought of, it is calculated to foster his self-conceit."

"Ben is not self-conceited," said Mrs. Barclay, ready to resent any slur upon her boy. "He has excellent business capacity, and if he were older I should not need to ask favors of anyone."

"You are a mother, and naturally set an exaggerated estimate upon your son's ability, which, I presume, is respectable, but probably not more. However, let that pass. I did not call to discuss Ben but to inquire whether you had not thought better of the matter we discussed the other evening."

"I never shall, Squire Davenport. When the time comes you can foreclose, if you like, but it will never be done with my consent."

"Ahem! Your consent will not be required."

"And let me tell you, Squire Davenport, if you do this wicked thing, it won't benefit you in the end."

Squire Davenport shrugged his shoulders.

"I am not at all surprised to find you so unreasonable, Mrs. Barclay," he said. "It's the way with women. I should be glad if you would come to look upon the matter in a different light; but I cannot sacrifice my own interests in any event. The law is on my side."

"The law may be on your side, but the law upholds a great deal that is oppressive and cruel."

"A curious set of laws we should have if women made them," said the squire.

"They would not bear so heavily upon the poor as they do now."

"Well, I won't stop to discuss the matter. If you come to entertain different views about the house, send word by Ben, and we will arrange the details without delay. Mr. Kirk is anxious to move his family as soon as possible, and would like to secure the house at once."

"He will have to wait three months at least," said Mrs. Barclay coldly. "For that time, I believe the law protects me."

"You are right there; but at the end of that tine you cannot expect as liberal terms as we are now prepared to offer you."

"Liberal!" repeated the widow, in a meaning tone.

"So I regard it," said the squire stiffly. "Good-evening."

An hour later Mrs. Barclay's reflections were broken in upon by the ominous clang of the engine bell. This is a sound which always excites alarm in a country village.

"Where's the fire?" she asked anxiously, of a boy who was running by the house.

"It's Crawford's store!" was the startling reply. "It's blazin' up like anything. Guess it'll have to go."

"I hope Ben'll keep out of danger," thought Mrs. Barclay, as she hurriedly took her shawl and bonnet and started for the scene of excitement.

CHAPTER XIV

BEN SHOWS HIMSELF A HERO

A fire in a country village, particularly where the building is a prominent one, is sure to attract a large part of the resident population. Men, women, and children, as well as the hook and ladder company, hurried to the scene of conflagration. Everybody felt a personal interest in Crawford's. It was the great emporium which provided all the families in the village with articles of prime and secondary necessity. If Paris can be called France, then Crawford's might be called Pentonville.

"Crawford's on fire!" exclaimed old Captain Manson. "Bless my soul! It cannot be true. Where's my cane?"

"You don't mean to say you're goin' to the fire, father?" asked his widowed daughter in surprise, for the captain had bowed beneath the weight of eighty-six winters, and rarely left the domestic hearth.

"Do you think I'd stay at home when Crawford's was a-burning?" returned the captain.

"But remember, father, you ain't so young as you used to be. You might catch your death of cold."

Horatio Alger, Jr.

"What! at a fire?" exclaimed the old man, laughing at his own joke.

"You know what I mean. It's dreadfully imprudent. Why, I wouldn't go myself."

"Shouldn't think you would, at your time of life!" retorted her father, chuckling.

So the old man emerged into the street, and hurried as fast as his unsteady limbs would allow, to the fire.

"How did it catch?" the reader will naturally ask.

The young man who was the only other salesman besides Ben and the proprietor, had gone down cellar smoking a cigar. In one corner was a heap of shavings and loose papers. A spark from his cigar must have fallen there. Had he noticed it, with prompt measures the incipient fire might have been extinguished. But he went up stairs with the kerosene, which he had drawn for old Mrs. Watts, leaving behind him the seeds of destruction. Soon the flames, arising, caught the wooden flooring of the upper store. The smell of the smoke notified Crawford and his clerks of the impending disaster. When the door communicating with the basement was opened, a stifling smoke issued forth and the crackling of the fire was heard.

"Run, Ben; give the alarm!" called Mr. Crawford, pale with dismay and apprehension. It was no time then to inquire how the fire caught. There was only time to save as much of the stock as possible, since it was clear that the fire had gained too great a headway to be put out.

Ben lost no time, and in less than ten minutes the engine, which, fortunately, was housed only ten rods away, was on the ground. Though it was impossible to save the store, the fire might be prevented from spreading. A band of earnest workers aided Crawford in saving his stock. A large part, of course, must be sacrificed; but, perhaps, a quarter was saved.

All at once a terrified whisper spread from one to another:

"Mrs. Morton's children! Where are they? They must be in the third story."

A poor woman, Mrs. Morton, had been allowed, with her two children, to enjoy, temporarily, two rooms in the third story. She had gone to a farmer's two miles away to do some work, and her children, seven and nine years of age, had remained at home. They seemed doomed to certain death.

But, even as the inquiry went from lip to lip, the children appeared. They had clambered out of a third story window upon the sloping roof of the rear ell, and, pale and dismayed, stood in sight of the shocked and terrified crowd, shrieking for help!

"A ladder! A ladder!" exclaimed half a dozen.

But there was no ladder at hand - none nearer than Mr. Parmenter's, five minutes' walk away. While a messenger was getting it the fate of the children would be decided.

"Tell 'em to jump!" exclaimed Silas Carver.

Horatio Alger, Jr.

"They'd break their necks, you fool!" returned his wife.

"Better do that than be burned up!" said the old man.

No one knew what to do - no one but Ben Barclay.

He seized a coil of rope, and with a speed which surprised even himself, climbed up a tall oak tree, whose branches overshadowed the roof of the ell part. In less than a minute he found himself on a limb just over the children. To the end of the rope was fastened a strong iron hook.

Undismayed by his own danger, Ben threw his rope, though he nearly lost his footing while he was doing it, and with an aim so precise that the hook caught in the smaller girl's dress.

"Hold on to the rope, Jennie, if you can!" he shouted.

The girl obeyed him instinctively.

Drawing the cord hand over hand, the little girl swung clear, and was lowered into the arms of Ebenezer Strong, who detached the hook.

"Save the other, Ben!" shouted a dozen.

Ben needed no spur to further effort.

Again he threw the hook, and this time the older girl, comprehending what was required, caught the rope and swung off the roof, scarcely in time, for her clothing had caught fire. But when she reached the ground ready hands extinguished it and the crowd of anxious spectators breathed more freely, as Ben, throwing down the rope, rapidly descended the tree and stood once more in safety, having saved two lives.

Just then it was that the poor mother, almost frantic with fear, arrived on the ground.

"Where are my darlings? Who will save them?" she exclaimed, full of anguish, yet not comprehending that they were out of peril.

"They are safe, and here is the brave boy who saved their lives," said Ebenezer Strong.

"God bless you, Ben Barclay!" exclaimed the poor mother. "You have saved my life as well as theirs, for I should have died if they had burned."

Ben scarcely heard her, for one and another came up to shake his hand and congratulate him upon his brave deed. Our young hero was generally self-possessed, but he hardly knew how to act when he found himself an object of popular ovation.

"Somebody else would have done it if I hadn't," he said modestly.

"You are the only one who had his wits about him," said Seth Jones. "No one thought of the rope till you climbed the tree. We were all looking for a ladder and there was none to be had nearer than Mr. Parmenter's."

"I wouldn't have thought of it myself if I hadn't read in a daily paper of something like it," said Ben.

"Ben," said Mr. Crawford, "I'd give a thousand dollars to have done what you did. You have shown yourself a hero."

"Oh, Ben, how frightened I was when I saw you on the branch just over the burning building," said a well-known voice.

Turning, Ben saw it was his mother who spoke.

"Well, it's all right now, mother," he said, smiling. "You are not sorry I did it?"

"Sorry! I am proud of you."

"I am not proud of my hands," said Ben. "Look at them."

They were chafed and bleeding, having been lacerated by his rapid descent from the tree.

"Come home, Ben, and let me put some salve on them. How they must pain you!"

"Wait till the fire is all over, mother."

The gallant firemen did all they could, but the store was doomed. They could only prevent it from extending. In half an hour the engine was taken back, and Ben went home with his mother.

"It's been rather an exciting evening, mother," said Ben. "I rather think I shall have to find a new place."

CHAPTER XV

BEN LOSES HIS PLACE

Ben did not find himself immediately out of employment. The next morning Mr. Crawford commenced the work of ascertaining what articles he had saved, and storing them. Luckily there was a vacant store which had once been used for a tailor's shop, but had been unoccupied for a year or more. This he hired, and at once removed his goods to it. But he did not display his usual energy. He was a man of over sixty, and no longer possessed the enterprise and ambition which had once characterized him. Besides, he was very comfortably off, or would be when he obtained the insurance money.

"I don't know what I shall do," he said, when questioned. "I was brought up on a farm, and I always meant to end my days on one. Perhaps now is as well any time, since my business is broken up."

This came to the ears of Squire Davenport, who was always keen-scented for a bargain. His wife's cousin, Mr. Kirk, who has already been introduced to the reader, had, in his earlier days, served as a clerk in a country store. He had no capital, to be sure, but the squire had plenty. It occurred to him as a good plan to buy out the business himself, hire Kirk on a salary to

Horatio Alger, Jr.

conduct it, and so add considerably to his already handsome income. He sent for Kirk, ascertained that he was not only willing, but anxious, to manage the business, and then he called on Mr. Crawford.

It is unnecessary to detail the negotiations that ensued. It was Squire Davenport's wish to obtain the business as cheaply as possible. The storekeeper, however, had his own estimate of its worth, and the squire was obliged to add considerable to his first offer. In the end, however, he secured it on advantageous terms, and Mr. Crawford now felt able to carry out the plan he had long had in view.

It was in the evening, a week after the fire, that the bargain was struck, and Ben was one of the first to hear of it.

When he came to work early the next morning he found his employer in the store before him, which was not usual.

"You are early, Mr. Crawford," he said, in evident surprise.

"Yes, Ben," was the reply. "I can afford to come early for a morning or two, as I shall soon be out of business."

"You haven't sold out, have you?" inquired Ben quickly.

"Yes; the bargain was struck last evening."

"How soon do you leave the store?"

"In three days. It will take that time to make up my accounts."

"I am sorry," said Ben, "for I suppose I shall have to retire, too."

"I don't know about that, Ben. Very likely my successor may want you."

"That depends on who he is. Do you mind telling me, or is it a secret?"

"Oh, no; it will have to come out, of course. Squire Davenport has bought the business."

"The squire isn't going to keep the store, is he?" asked Ben, in amazement.

"No; though he will, no doubt, supervise it. He will employ a manager."

"Do you know who is to be the manager, Mr. Crawford?"

"Some connection of his named Kirk."

Ben whistled.

"Do you know him?" the storekeeper was led to inquire.

"I have not seen him, but he called with the squire on my mother," said Ben significantly.

"I shall be glad to recommend you to him."

"It will be of no use, Mr. Crawford," answered Ben, in a decided tone. "I know he wouldn't employ me, nor would I work for him if he would. Neither he nor the squire is a friend of mine."

"I did not dream of this, Ben. I am sorry if the step I have taken is going to deprive you of employment," said Mr. Crawford, who was a kind-hearted man, and felt a sincere interest in his young clerk.

"Never mind, Mr. Crawford, I am not cast down. There will be other openings for me. I am young, strong, and willing to work, and I am sure I shall find something to do."

"That's right, Ben. Cheer up, and if I hear of any good chance, rest assured that I will let you know of it."

Tom Davenport was not long in hearing of his father's bargain. He heard it with unfeigned pleasure, for it occurred to him at once that Ben, for whom he had a feeling of hatred, by no means creditable to him, would be thrown out of employment.

"Promise me, pa, that you won't employ Ben Barclay," he said.

"I have no intention of employing that boy," said his father. "Mr. Kirk has a son of his own, about Ben's age, and will, no doubt, put him into the store, unless you should choose to go in and learn the business."

"What! I become a store boy!" exclaimed Tom, in disgust. "No, thank you. I might be willing to become salesman in a large establishment in the city, but I don't care to go into a country grocery."

"It wouldn't do you any harm," said the squire, who was not quite so high-minded as his son. "However, I merely mentioned it as something you could do if you chose."

"Bah! I don't choose it," said Tom decidedly.

"Well, well; you won't have to do it."

"It would put me on a level with Ben Barclay, if I stepped into his shoes. Won't he be down in the month when he hears he has lost his place?" and Tom chuckled at the thought.

"That is no concern of mine," said the squire. "I suppose he can hire out to a farmer."

"Just the business for him", said Tom, "unless he should prefer to go to New York and set up as a bootblack. I believe I'll suggest that to him!"

"Probably he won't thank you for the suggestion."

"I guess not. He's as proud as he is poor. It's amusing to see what airs he puts on."

Squire Davenport, however, was not so much interested in that phase of the subject as Tom, and did not reply.

"I think I'll go down street," thought Tom. "Perhaps I may come across Ben. I shall enjoy seeing how he takes it."

Tom had scarcely walked a hundred yards when he met, not the one of whom he had thought, but another to whom he felt glad to speak on the same subject. This was Rose Gardiner, the prettiest girl in the village, who had already deeply offended Tom by accepting Ben as her escort from the magical entertainment in place of him. He had made advances since, being desirous of ousting Ben from his position of favorite, but the young lady had treated him coldly, much to his anger and mortification.

"Good-morning, Miss Rose," said Tom.

"Good-morning," answered Rose civilly.

"Have you heard the news?"

"To what news do you refer?"

"Crawford has sold out his business."

"Indeed!" said Rose, in surprise; "who has bought it?"

"My father. Of course, he won't keep store himself. He will put in a connection of ours, Mr. Kirk."

"This is news, indeed! Where is Mr. Crawford going?"

"I don't know, I'm sure. I thought you'd be more apt to inquire about somebody else?"

"I am not good at guessing enigmas," said Rose.

"Your friend, Ben Barclay," returned Tom, with a sneer. "Father won't have him in the store!"

"Oh, I see; you are going to take his place," said Rose mischievously.

"I? What do you take me for?" said Tom, haughtily. "I suppose Ben Barclay will have to go to work on a farm."

"That is a very honorable employment," said Rose calmly.

"Yes; he can be a hired man when he grows up. Perhaps, though, he will prefer to go to the city and become a bootblack."

"Ben ought to be very much obliged to you for the interest you feel in his welfare," said Rose, looking steadily and scornfully at Tom. "Good-morning."

"She feels sore about it," thought Tom complacently. "She won't be quite so ready to accept Ben's attentions when he is a farm laborer."

Tom, however, did not understand Rose Gardiner. She was a girl of good sense, and her estimate of others was founded on something else than social position.

CHAPTER XVI

BEN FINDS TEMPORARY EMPLOYMENT

"Oh, Ben, what shall we do?" exclaimed Mrs. Barclay, when she heard Mr. Crawford had sold out his business.

"We'll get along somehow, mother. Something will be sure to turn up."

Ben spoke more cheerfully than he felt. He knew very well that Pentonville presented scarcely any field for a boy, unless he was willing to work on a farm. Now, Ben had no objections to farm labor, provided he had a farm of his own, but at the rate such labor was paid in Pentonville, there was very little chance of ever rising above the position of a "hired man," if he once adopted the business. Our young hero felt that this would not satisfy him. He was enterprising and ambitious, and wanted to be a rich man some day.

Money is said, by certain moralists, to be the root of all evil. The love of money, if carried too far, may indeed lead to evil, but it is a natural ambition in any boy or man to wish to raise himself above poverty. The wealth of Amos Lawrence and Peter Cooper was a source of blessing to mankind, yet each started as a poor boy, and neither would have become rich if he had not striven hard to become so.

When Ben made this cheerful answer his mother shook her head sadly. She was not so hopeful as Ben, and visions of poverty presented themselves before her mind.

"I don't see what you can find to do in Pentonville, Ben," she said.

"I can live a while without work while I am looking around, mother," Ben answered. "We have got all that money I brought from New York yet."

"It won't last long," said his mother despondently.

"It will last till I can earn some more," answered Ben hopefully.

Ben was about to leave the house when a man in a farmer's frock, driving a yoke of oxen, stopped his team in the road, and turned in at the widow's gate.

It was Silas Greyson, the owner of a farm just out of the village.

"Did you want to see mother?" asked Ben.

"No, I wanted to see you, Benjamin," answered Greyson. "I hear you've left the store."

"The store has changed hands, and the new storekeeper don't want me."

"Do you want a job?"

"What is it, Mr. Greyson?" Ben replied, answering one question with another.

"I'm goin' to get in wood for the winter from my wood lot for about a week," said the farmer, "and I want help. Are you willin' to hire out for a week?"

"What'll you pay me?" asked Ben.

"I'll keep you, and give you a cord of wood. Your mother'll find it handy. I'm short of money, and calc'late wood'll be just as good pay."

Ben thought over the proposal, and answered: "I'd rather take my meals at home, Mr. Greyson, and if you'll make it two cords with that understanding, I'll agree to hire out to you."

"Ain't that rather high?" asked the farmer, hesitating.

"I don't think so."

Finally Silas Greyson agreed, and Ben promised to be on hand bright and early the next day. It may be stated here that wood was very cheap at Pentonville, so that Ben would not be overpaid.

There were some few things about the house which Ben wished to do for his mother before he went to work anywhere, and he thought this a good opportunity to do them. While in the store his time had been so taken up that he was unable to attend to them. He passed a busy day, therefore, and hardly went into the street.

Just at nightfall, as he was in the front yard, he was

rather surprised to see Tom Davenport open the gate and enter.

"What does he want, I wonder?" he thought, but he said, in a civil tone: "Good-evening, Tom."

"You're out of business, ain't you?" asked Tom abruptly.

"I'm not out of work at any rate!" answered Ben.

"Why, what work are you doing?" interrogated Tom, in evident disappointment.

"I've been doing some jobs about the house, for mother."

"That won't give you a living," said Tom disdainfully.

"Very true."

"Did you expect to stay in the store?" asked Tom.

"Not after I heard that your father had bought it," answered Ben quietly.

"My father's willing to give you work," said Tom.

"Is he?" asked Ben, very much surprised.

It occurred to him that perhaps he would have a chance to remain in the store after all, and for the present that would have suited him. Though he didn't like the squire, or Mr. Kirk, he felt that he had no right, in his present circumstances, to refuse any way to earn an honest living.

"Yes," answered Tom. "I told him he'd better hire you."

"You did!" exclaimed Ben, more and more amazed. "I didn't expect that. However, go on, if you please."

"He's got three cords of wood that he wants sawed and split," said Tom, "and as I knew how poor you were I thought it would be a good chance for you."

You might have thought from Tom's manner that he was a young lord, and Ben a peasant. Ben was not angry, but amused.

"It is true," he said. "I am not rich; still, I am not as poor as you think."

He happened to have in his pocketbook the money he had brought from New York, and this he took from his pocket and displayed to the astonished Tom.

"Where did you get that money?" asked Tom, surprised and chagrined.

"I got it honestly. You see we can hold out a few days. However, I may be willing to accept the job you offer me. How much is your father willing to pay me?"

"He is willing to give you forty cents a day."

"How long does he expect me to work for that?"

"Ten hours."

"That is four cents an hour, and hard work at that. I am much obliged to you and him, Tom, for your liberal offer, but I can't accept it."

"You'll see the time when you'll be glad to take such a job," said Tom, who was personally disappointed that he would not be able to exhibit Ben as his father's hired dependent.

"You seem to know all about it, Tom," answered Ben. "I shall be at work all next week, at much higher pay, for Silas Greyson."

"How much does he pay you?"

"That is my private business, and wouldn't interest you."

"You're mighty independent for a boy in your position."

"Very likely. Won't you come in?"

"No," answered Tom ungraciously; "I've wasted too much time here already."

"I understand Tom's object in wanting to hire me," thought Ben. "He wants to order me around. Still, if the squire had been willing to pay a decent price, I would have accepted the job. I won't let pride stand in the way of my supporting mother and myself."

This was a sensible and praiseworthy resolution, as I hope my young readers will admit. I don't think much of the pride that is willing to let others suffer in order that it may be gratified.

Ben worked a full week for Farmer Greyson, and

Horatio Alger, Jr.

helped unload the two cords of wood, which were his wages, in his mother's yard. Then there were two days of idleness, which made him anxious. On the second day, just after supper, he met Rose Gardiner coming from the post office.

"Have you any correspondents in New York, Ben?" she asked.

"What makes you ask, Rose?"

Because the postmaster told me there was a letter for you by this evening's mail. It was mailed in New York, and was directed in a lady's hand. I hope you haven't been flirting with any New York ladies, Mr. Barclay."

"The only lady I know in New York is at least fifty years old," answered Ben, smiling.

"That is satisfactory," answered Rose solemnly. "Then I won't be jealous."

"What can the letter be?" thought Ben. "I hope it contains good news."

He hurried to the post office in a fever of excitement.

CHAPTER XVII

WHAT THE LETTER CONTAINED

"I hear there is a letter for me, Mr. Brown," said Ben to the postmaster, who was folding the evening papers, of which he received a parcel from the city by the afternoon train.

"Yes, Ben," answered the postmaster, smiling. "It appears to be from a lady in New York. You must have improved your time during your recent visit to the city."

"I made the acquaintance of one lady older than my mother," answered Ben. "I didn't flirt with her any."

"At any rate, I should judge that she became interested in you or she wouldn't write."

"I hope she did, for she is very wealthy," returned Ben.

The letter was placed in his hands, and he quickly tore it open.

Something dropped from it.

"What is that?" asked the postmaster.

Horatio Alger, Jr.

Ben stooped and picked it up, and, to his surprise, discovered that it was a ten-dollar bill.

"That's a correspondent worth having," said Mr. Brown jocosely. "Can't you give me a letter of introduction?"

Ben didn't answer, for he was by this time deep the letter. We will look over his shoulder and read it with him. It ran thus:

"No. -- Madison Avenue,
New York, October 5.

"My Dear Young Friend:

"Will you come to New York and call upon me? I have a very pleasant remembrance of you and the service you did me recently, and think I can employ you in other ways, to our mutual advantage. I am willing to pay you a higher salary than you are receiving in your country home, besides providing you with a home in my own house. I inclose ten dollars for expenses. Yours, with best wishes,

"Helen Hamilton"

Ben's heart beat with joyful excitement as he read this letter. It could not have come at a better time, for, as we know, he was out of employment, and, of course, earning nothing.

"Well, Ben," said the postmaster, whose curiosity was excited, is it good news?"

"I should say it was," said Ben emphatically. "I am offered a good situation in New York."

"You don't say so! How much are offered?"

"I am to get more than Mr. Crawford paid me and board in a fine house besides - a brownstone house on Madison Avenue."

"Well, I declare! You are in luck," ejaculated Mr. Brown. "What are you to do?"

"That's more than I know. Here is the letter, if you like to read it."

"It reads well. She must be a generous lady. But what will your mother say?"

"That's what I want to know," said Ben, looking suddenly sober. "I hate to leave her, but it is for my good."

"Mothers are self-sacrificing when the interests of their children are concerned."

"I know that," said Ben promptly; "and I've got one of the best mothers going."

"So you have. Every one likes and respects Mrs. Barclay."

Any boy, who is worth anything, likes to hear his mother praised, and Ben liked Mr. Brown better for this tribute to the one whom he loved best on earth. He was not slow in making his way home. He went at once to the kitchen, where his mother was engaged in mixing bread.

"What's the matter, Ben? You look excited,"

Horatio Alger, Jr.

said Mrs. Barkley.

"So I am, mother. I am offered a position."

"Not in the store?"

"No; it is in New York."

"In New York!" repeated his mother, in a troubled voice. "It would cost you all you could make to pay your board in some cheap boarding house. If it were really going to be for your own good, I might consent to part with you, but - "

"Read that letter, mother," said Ben. "You will see that I shall have an elegant home and a salary besides. It is a chance in a thousand."

Mrs. Barclay read the letter carefully.

"Can I go, mother?" Ben asked anxiously.

"It will be a sacrifice for me to part with you," returned his mother slowly; "but I agree with you that it is a rare chance, and I should be doing wrong to stand in the way of your good fortune. Mrs. Hamilton must have formed a very good opinion of you."

"She may be disappointed in me," said Ben modestly.

"I don't think she will," said Mrs. Barclay, with a proud and affectionate glance at her boy. "You have always been a good son, and that is the best of recommendations."

"I am afraid you are too partial, mother. I shall hate to

leave you alone."

"I can bear loneliness if I know you are prospering, Ben."

"And it will only be for a time, mother. When I am a young man and earning a good income, I shall want you to come and live with me."

"All in good time, Ben. How soon do you want to go?"

"I think it better to lose no time, mother. You know I have no work to keep me in Pentonville."

"But it will take two or three days to get your clothes ready."

"You can send them to me by express. I shall send you the address."

Mrs. Barclay was a fond mother, but she was also a sensible woman. She felt that Ben was right, and, though it seemed very sudden, she gave him her permission to start the next morning. Had she objected strenuously, Ben would have given up his plan, much as he desired it, for he felt that his mother had the strongest claims upon him, and he would not have been willing to run counter to her wishes.

"Where are you going, Ben?" asked his mother, as Ben put on his hat and moved toward the door.

"I thought I would like to call on Rose Gardiner to say good-by," answered Ben.

"Quite right, my son. Rose is a good friend of yours,

Horatio Alger, Jr.

and an excellent girl"

"I say ditto to that, mother," Ben answered warmly.

I am not going to represent Ben as being in love - he was too young for that - but, like many boys of his age, he felt a special attraction in the society of one young girl. His good taste was certainly not at fault in his choice of Rose Gardiner, who, far from being frivolous and fashionable, was a girl of sterling traits, who was not above making herself useful in the household of which she formed a part.

On his way to the home of Rose Gardiner, Ben met Tom Davenport.

"How are you getting along?" asked Tom, not out of interest, but curiosity.

"Very well, thank you."

"Have you got through helping the farmer?"

"Yes."

"It was a very long job. Have you thought better of coming to saw wood for father?"

"No; I have thought worse of it," answered Ben, smiling.

"You are too proud. Poor and proud don't agree."

"Not at all. I would have had no objection to the work. It was the pay I didn't like."

"You can't earn more than forty cents a day at anything else."

"You are mistaken. I am going to New York to-morrow to take a place, where I get board and considerable more money besides."

"Is that true?" asked Tom, looking as if he had lost his best friend.

"Quite so. The party inclosed ten dollars to pay my expenses up to the city."

"He must be a fool."

"Thank you. It happens to be a lady."

"What are you to do?"

"I don't know yet. I am sure I shall be well paid. I must ask you to excuse me now, as I am going to call on Rose Gardiner to bid her good-by."

"I dare say she would excuse you," said Tom, with a sneer.

"Perhaps so; but I wouldn't like to go without saying good-by."

"At any rate, he will be out of my way," thought Tom, "and I can monopolize Rose. I'm glad he's going."

He bade Ben an unusually civil good-night at this thought occurred to him.

CHAPTER XVIII

FAREWELL TO PENTONVILLE

"I have come to say good-by, Rose," said Ben, as the young lady made her appearance.

"Good-by!" repeated Rose, in surprise. "Why, where are you going?"

"To New York."

"But you are coming back again?"

"I hope so, but only for a visit now and then. I am offered a position in the city."

"Isn't that rather sudden?" said Rose, after a pause.

Ben explained how he came to be offered employment.

"I am to receive higher pay than I did here, and a home besides," he added, in a tone of satisfaction. "Don't you think I am lucky?"

"Yes, Ben, and I rejoice in your good fortune; but I shall miss you so much," said Rose frankly.

"I am glad of that," returned Ben. "I hoped you would

miss me a little. You'll go and see mother now and then, won't you? She will feel very lonely."

"You may be sure I will. It is a pity you have to go away. A great many will be sorry."

"I know someone who won't."

"Who is that?"

"Tom Davenport."

Rose smiled. She had a little idea why Tom would not regret Ben's absence.

"Tom could be spared, as well as not," she said.

"He is a strong admirer of yours, I believe," said Ben mischievously.

"I don't admire him," retorted Rose, with a little toss of her head.

Ben heard this with satisfaction, for though he was too young to be a lover, he did have a strong feeling of attraction toward Rose, and would have been sorry to have Tom step into his place.

As Ben was preparing to go, Rose said, "Wait a minute, Ben."

She left the room and went upstairs, but returned almost immediately, with a small knit purse.

"Won't you accept this, Ben?" she said. "I just finished it yesterday. It will remind you of me when you are away."

"Thank you, Rose. I shall need nothing to keep you in my remembrance, but I will value it for your sake."

"I hope you will be fortunate and fill it very soon, Ben."

So the two parted on the most friendly terms, and the next day Ben started for New York in the highest of spirits.

After purchasing his ticket, he gave place to Squire Davenport, who also called for a ticket to New York. Now, it so happened that the squire had not seen Tom since the interview of the latter with our hero, and was in ignorance of his good luck.

"Are you going to New York, Benjamin?" he asked, in surprise.

"Yes, sir."

"Isn't it rather extravagant for one in your circumstances?"

"Yes, sir; if I had no object in view."

"Have you any business in the city?"

"Yes, sir; I am going to take a place."

Squire Davenport was still more surprised, and asked particulars. These Ben readily gave, for he was quite elated by his good fortune.

"Oh, that's it, is it?" said the squire contemptuously. "I thought you might have secured a position in some business house. This lady probably wants you to answer the doorbell and clean the knives, or something of that sort."

"I am sure she does not," said Ben, indignant and mortified.

"You'll find I am right," said the squire confidently. "Young man, I can't congratulate you on your prospects. You would have done as well to stay in Pentonville and work on my woodpile."

"Whatever work I may do in New York, I shall be a good deal better paid for than here," retorted Ben.

Squire Davenport shrugged his shoulders, and began to read the morning paper. To do him justice, he only said what he thought when he predicted to Ben that he would be called upon to do menial work.

"The boy won't be in so good spirits a week hence," he thought. "However, that is not my affair. There is no doubt that I shall get possession of his mother's house when the three months are up, and I don't at all care where he and his mother go. If they leave Pentonville I shall be very well satisfied. I have no satisfaction in meeting either of them," and the squire frowned, as if some unpleasant thought had crossed his mind.

Nothing of note passed during the remainder of the journey. Ben arrived in New York, and at once took a conveyance uptown, and due time found himself, carpet-bag in hand, on the front steps of Mrs. Hamilton's house.

Horatio Alger, Jr.

He rang the bell, and the door was opened by a servant.

"She's out shopping," answered the girl, looking inquisitively at Ben's carpet-bag. "Will you leave a message for her?"

"I believe I am expected," said Ben, feeling a little awkward. "My name is Benjamin Barclay."

"Mrs. Hamilton didn't say anything about expecting any boy," returned the servant. "You can come in, if you like, and I'll call Mrs. Hill."

"I suppose that is the housekeeper," thought Ben.

"Very well," he answered. "I believe I will come in, as Mrs. Hamilton wrote me to come."

Ben left his bag in the front hall, and with his hat in his hand followed the servant into the handsomely-furnished drawing room.

"I wish Mrs. Hamilton had been here," he said to himself. "The girl seems to look at me suspiciously. I hope the housekeeper knows about my coming."

Ben sat down in an easy-chair beside a marble-topped center table, and waited for fifteen minutes before anyone appeared. He beguiled the time by looking over a handsomely illustrated book of views, but presently the door was pushed open and he looked up.

The newcomer was a spare, pale-faced woman, with a querulous expression, who stared coldly at our hero. It was clear that she was not glad to see him. "What can I do for you, young man?" she asked in a repellent tone.

"What a disagreeable-looking woman!" thought Ben. "I am sure we shall never be friends."

"Is Mrs. Hamilton expected in soon?" he asked.

"I really cannot say. She does not report to me how long she expects to be gone."

"Didn't she speak to you about expecting me?" asked Ben, feeling decidedly uncomfortable.

"Not a word!" was the reply.

"She wrote to me to come here, but perhaps she did not expect me so soon."

"If you have come here to collect a bill, or with any business errand, I can attend to you. I am Mrs. Hamilton's cousin."

"Thank you; it will be necessary for me to see Mrs. Hamilton."

"Then you may as well call in the afternoon, or some other day."

"That's pretty cool!" thought Ben. "That woman wants to get me out of the house, but I propose to 'hold the fort' till Mrs. Hamilton arrives."

"I thought you might know that I am going to stay here," said Ben.

"What!" exclaimed Mrs. Hill, in genuine surprise.

"Mrs. Hamilton has offered me a position, though I do

not know what the duties are to be, and am going to make my home here."

"Really this is too much!" said the pale-faced lady sternly. "Here, Conrad!" she called, going to the door.

A third party made his appearance on the scene, a boy who looked so much like Mrs. Hill that it was clear she was his mother. He was two inches taller than Ben, but looked pale and flabby.

"What's wanted, ma?" he said, staring at Ben.

"This young man has made a strange mistake. He says Mrs. Hamilton has sent for him and that he is going to live here.

"He's got cheek," exclaimed Conrad, continuing to stare at Ben.

"Tell him he'd better go!"

"You'd better go!" said the boy, like a parrot.

"Thank you," returned Ben, provoked, "but I mean to stay."

"Go and call a policeman, Conrad," said Mrs. Hill. "We'll see what he'll have to say then."

CHAPTER XIX

A COOL RECEPTION

"This isn't quite the reception I expected," thought Ben. He was provoked with the disagreeable woman who persisted in regarding and treating him as an intruder, but he was not nervous or alarmed. He knew that things would come right, and that Mrs. Hill and her promising son would see their mistake. He had half a mind to let Conrad call a policeman, and then turn the tables upon his foes. But, he knew that this would be disagreeable to Mrs. Hamilton, whose feelings he was bound to consider.

"Before you call a policeman," he said quietly, "it may be well for you to read this letter."

As he spoke handed Mrs. Hill the letter he had received from Mrs. Hamilton.

Mrs. Hill took the letter suspiciously, and glared over it. As she read, a spot of red glowed in each pallid check, and she bit her lips in annoyance.

"I don't understand it," she said slowly.

Ben did not feel called upon to explain what was perfectly intelligible. He saw that Mrs. Hill didn't want

Horatio Alger, Jr.

to understand it.

"What is it, ma?" asked Conrad, his curiosity aroused.

"You can read it for yourself, Conrad," returned his mother.

"Is he coming to live here?" ejaculated Conrad, astonished, indicating Ben with a jerk of his finger.

"If this letter is genuine," said Mrs. Hill, with at significant emphasis on the last word.

"If it is not, Mrs. Hamilton will be sure to tell you so," said Ben, provoked.

"Come out, Conrad; I want to speak to you," said his mother.

Without ceremony, they left Ben in the parlor alone, and withdrew to another part of the house, where they held a conference.

"What does it all mean, ma?" asked Conrad.

"It means that your prospects are threatened, my poor boy. Cousin Hamilton, who is very eccentric, has taken a fancy to this boy, and she is going to confer favors upon him at your expense. It is too bad!"

"I'd like to break his head!" said Conrad, scowling.

"It won't do, Conrad, to fight him openly. We must do what we can in an underhand way to undermine him with Cousin Hamilton. She ought to make you her heir, as she has no children of her own."

"I don't think she likes me," said the boy. "She only gives me two dollars a week allowance, and she scolded me the other day because she met me in the hall smoking a cigarette."

"Be sure not to offend her, Conrad. A great deal depends on it. Two dollars ought to answer for the present. When you are a young man, you may be in very different circumstances."

"I don't know about that," grumbled Conrad. "I may get two dollars a week then, but what's that?"

"You may be a wealthy man!" said his mother impressively. "Cousin Hamilton is not so healthy as she looks. I have a suspicion that her heart is affected. She might die suddenly."

"Do you really think so?" said Conrad eagerly.

"I think so. What you must try to do is to stand well with her, and get her to make her will in your favor. I will attend to that, if you will do as I tell you."

"She may make this boy her heir," said Conrad discontentedly. "Then where would I be?"

"She won't do it, if I can help it," said Mrs. Hill with an emphatic nod. "I will manage to make trouble between them. You will always be my first interest, my dear boy."

She made a motion to kiss her dear boy, but Conrad, who was by no means of an affectionate disposition, moved his head suddenly, with an impatient exclamation, "Oh, bother!"

A pained look came over the mother's face, for she loved her son, unattractive and disagreeable as he was, with a love the greater because she loved no one else in the world. Mother and son were selfish alike, but the son the more so, for he had not a spark of love for any human being.

"There's the bell!" said Mrs. Hill suddenly. "I do believe Cousin Hamilton has come. Now we shall find out whether this boy's story is true."

"Let's go downstairs, ma! I hope it's all a mistake and she'll send me for a policeman."

"I am afraid the boy's story is correct. But his day will be short."

When they reached the hall, Mrs. Hamilton had already been admitted to the house.

"There's a boy in the drawing room, Mrs. Hamilton," said Mrs. Hill, "who says he is to stay here - that you sent for him."

"Has he come already?" returned Mrs. Hamilton. "I am glad of it."

"Then you did send for him?"

"Of course. Didn't I mention it to you? I hardly expected he would come so soon."

She opened the door of the drawing room, and approached Ben, with extended hand and a pleasant smile.

"Welcome to New York, Ben," she said. "I hope I haven't kept you waiting long?"

"Not very long," answered Ben, shaking her hand.

"This is my cousin Mrs. Hill, who relieves me of part of my housekeeping care," continued Mrs. Hamilton, "and this is her son, Conrad. Conrad, this is a companion for you, Benjamin Barclay, who will be a new member of our small family."

"I hope you are well, Conrad," said Ben, with a smile, to the boy who but a short time before was going for a policeman to put him under arrest.

"I'm all right," said Conrad ungraciously.

"Really, Cousin Hamilton, this is a surprise" said Mrs. Hill. "You are quite kind to provide Conrad with a companion, but I don't think he felt the need of any, except his mother - and you."

Mrs. Hamilton laughed. She saw that neither Mrs. Hill nor Conrad was glad to see Ben, and this was only what she expected, and, indeed, this was the chief reason why she had omitted to mention Ben's expected arrival.

"You give me too much credit," she said, "if you think I invited this young gentleman here solely as a companion to Conrad. I shall have some writing and accounts for him to attend to."

"I am sure Conrad would have been glad to serve you in that way, Cousin Hamilton," said Mrs. Hill. "I am sorry you did not give him the first chance."

"Conrad wouldn't have suited me," said Mrs. Hamilton bluntly.

"Perhaps I may not be competent," suggested Ben modestly.

"We can tell better after trying you," said his patroness. "As for Conrad, I have obtained a position for him. He is to enter the offices of Jones & Woodhull, on Pearl Street, to-morrow. You will take an early breakfast, Conrad, for it will be necessary for you to be at the office at eight o'clock."

"How much am I to get?" asked Conrad.

"Four dollars a week. I shall let you have all this in lieu of the weekly allowance I pay you, but will provide you with clothing, as heretofore, so that this will keep you liberally supplied with pocket money."

"Conrad's brow cleared. He was lazy, and did not enjoy going to work, but the increase of his allowance would be satisfactory.

"And now, Ben, Mrs. Hill will kindly show you your room. It is the large hall bedroom on the third floor. When you have unpacked your valise, and got to feel at home, come downstairs, and we will have a little conversation upon business. You will find me in the sitting room, on the next floor."

"Thank you," said Ben politely, and he followed the pallid cousin upstairs. He was shown into a handsomely furnished room, bright and cheerful.

"This is a very pleasant room," he said.

"You won't occupy it long!" said Mrs. Hill to herself. "No one will step into my Conrad's place, if I can help it."

CHAPTER XX

ENTERING UPON HIS DUTIES

When Ben had taken out his clothing from his valise and put it away in the drawers of the handsome bureau which formed a part of the furniture of his room, he went downstairs, and found his patroness in a cozy sitting room, on the second floor. It was furnished, Ben could not help thinking, more as if it were designed for a gentleman than a lady. In one corner was a library table, with writing materials, books, and papers upon it, and an array of drawers on either side of the central part.

"Come right in, Ben," said Mrs. Hamilton, who was seated at the table. "We will talk of business."

This Ben was quite willing to do. He was anxious to know what were to be his duties, that he might judge whether he was competent to discharge them.

"Let me tell you, to begin with," said his patroness, "that I am possessed of considerable wealth, as, indeed, you may have judged by way of living. I have no children, unfortunately, and being unwilling, selfishly, to devote my entire means to my own use exclusively, I try to help others in a way that I think most suitable. Mrs. Hill, who acts as my housekeeper, is a cousin, who made a poor marriage, and was left penniless. I have given a home to her and her son."

"I don't think Mrs. Hill likes my being here," said Ben.

"You are, no doubt, right. She is foolish enough to be jealous because I do not bestow all my favors upon her."

"I think she will look upon me as a rival of her son."

"I expected she would. Perhaps she will learn, after a while, that I can be a friend to you and him both, though, I am free to admit, I have never been able to take any fancy to Conrad, nor, indeed, was his mother a favorite with me. But for her needy circumstances, she is, perhaps, the last of my relatives that I would invite to become a member of my household. However, to come to business: My money is invested in various ways. Besides the ordinary forms of investment, stocks, bonds, and mortgages, I have set up two or three young men, whom I thought worthy, in business, and require them to send in monthly statements of their business to me. You see, therefore, that I have more or less to do with accounts. I never had much taste for figures, and it struck me that I might relieve myself of considerable drudgery if I could obtain your assistance, under my supervision, of course. I hope you have a taste for figures?"

"Arithmetic and algebra are my favorite studies," said Ben promptly.

"I am glad of it. Of course, I did not know that, but had you not been well versed in accounts, I meant to send you to a commercial school to qualify you for the duties I wished to impose upon you."

"I don't think it will be necessary," answered Ben. "I have taken lessons in bookkeeping at home, and, though it seems like boasting, I was better in mathematics than any of my schoolfellows."

"I am so glad to hear that. Can you write well?"

"Shall I write something for you?"

"Do so."

Mrs. Hamilton vacated her place, and Ben, sitting at the desk, wrote two or three copies from remembrance.

"Very well, indeed!" said his patroness approvingly. "I see that in engaging you I have made no mistake."

Ben's cheek flushed with pleasure, and he was eager to enter upon his new duties. But he could not help wondering why he had been selected when Conrad was already in the house, and unemployed. He ventured to say:

"Would you mind telling me why you did not employ Conrad, instead of sending for me?"

"There are two good and sufficient reasons: Conrad is not competent for such an office; and secondly, I should not like to have the boy about me as much as he would need to be. I have obtained for him a position out of the house. One question remains to be considered: How much wages do you expect?"

"I would prefer to leave that to you, Mrs. Hamilton. I

cannot expect high pay."

"Will ten dollars a week be adequate?"

"I can't earn as much money as that," said Ben, in surprise.

"Perhaps not, and yet I am not sure. If you suit me, it will be worth my while to pay you as much."

"But Conrad will only receive four dollars a week. Won't he be angry?"

"Conrad is not called upon to support his mother, as I understand you are."

"You are very kind to think of that, Mrs. Hamilton."

"I want to be kind to you, Ben," said his patroness with a pleasant smile.

"When shall I commence my duties?"

"Now. You will copy this statement into the ledger you see here. Before doing so, will you look over and verify the figures?"

Ben was soon hard at work. He was interested in his work, and the time slipped fast. After an hour and a half had passed, Mrs. Hamilton said:

"It is about time for lunch, and I think there will be no more to do to-day. Are you familiar with New York?"

"No, I have spent very little time in the city."

"You will, no doubt, like to look about. We have dinner at six sharp. You will be on tine?"

"I will be sure to be here."

"That reminds me - have you a watch?"

Ben shook his head.

"I thought it might be so. I have a good silver watch, which I have no occasion for."

Mrs. Hamilton left the room, and quickly returned with a neat silver hunting-case watch, with a guilt chain.

"This is yours, Ben," she said, "if you like it."

"Do you give it to me?" asked Ben joyously. He had only expected that it would be loaned to him.

"Yes, I give it to you, and I hope you will find it useful."

"How can I thank you, Mrs. Hamilton, for your kindness?"

"You are more grateful than Conrad. I gave him one just like it, and he was evidently dissatisfied became it was not gold. When you are older the gold watch may come."

"I am very well pleased with the silver watch, for I have long wanted one, but did not see any way of obtaining it."

"You are wise in having moderate desires, Ben. But

there goes the lunch bell. You may want to wash your hands. When you have done so come down to the dining room, in the rear of the sitting room."

Mrs. Hill and Conrad were already seated at the table when Ben descended.

"Take a seat opposite Conrad, Ben," said Mrs. Hamilton, who was sitting at one end of the table.

The lunch was plain but substantial, and Ben, who had taken an early breakfast, enjoyed it.

"I suppose we shall not have Conrad at lunch to-morrow?" said Mrs. Hamilton. "He will be at the store."

Conrad made a grimace. He world have enjoyed his freedom better.

"I won't have much of my four dollars left if I have to pay for lunch," he said in a surly tone.

"You shall have a reasonable allowance for that purpose."

"I suppose Mr. Barclay will lunch at home," said Mrs. Hill.

"Certainly, since his work will be here. He is to be my home clerk, and will keep my accounts."

"You needn't have gone out of the house for a clerk, Cousin Hamilton. I am sure Conrad would have been glad of the work."

"It will be better for Conrad to learn business in a larger establishment," said Mrs. Hamilton quietly.

This was a new way of looking at it, and helped to reconcile Mrs. Hill to an arrangement which at first had disappointed her.

"Have you any engagements this afternoon, Conrad?" asked Mrs. Hamilton. "Ben will have nothing to do, and you could show him the city."

"I've got an engagement with a fellow," said Conrad hastily.

"I can find my way about alone, thank you," said Ben. "I won't trouble Conrad."

"Very well. This evening, however, Ben, I think you may enjoy going to the theater. Conrad can accompany you, unless he has another engagement."

"I'll go with him," said Conrad, more graciously, for he was fond of amusements.

"Then we will all meet at dinner, and you two young gentlemen can leave in good time for the theater."

CHAPTER XXI

AT THE THEATER

After dinner, Ben and Conrad started to walk to the theater. The distance was about a mile, but in the city there is so much always to be seen that one does not think of distance.

Conrad, who was very curious to ascertain Ben's status in the household, lost no time in making inquiries.

"What does my aunt find for you to do?" he asked.

It may be remarked, by the way, that no such relationship ever existed between them, but Mrs. Hill and her son thought politic to make the relationship seem as close as possible, as it would, perhaps, increase their apparent claim upon their rich relative.

Ben answered the question.

"You'll have a stupid time," said Conrad. "All the same, she ought to have given the place to me. How much does she pay you?"

Ben hesitated, for he knew that his answer would make his companion discontented.

Horatio Alger, Jr.

"I am not sure whether I am at liberty to tell," he answered, with hesitation.

"There isn't any secret about it, is there?" said Conrad sharply.

No, I suppose not. I am to receive ten dollars a week."

"Ten dollars a week!" ejaculated Conrad, stopping short in the street.

"Yes."

"And I get but four! That's a shame!"

"I shall really have no more than you, Conrad. I have a mother to provide for, and I shall send home six dollars a week regularly."

"That doesn't make any difference!" exclaimed Conrad, in excitement. "It's awfully mean of aunt to treat you so much better than she does me."

"You mustn't say that to me," said Ben. "She has been kind to us both, and I don't like to hear anything said against her."

"You're not going to tell her?" said Conrad suspiciously.

"Certainly not," said Ben indignantly. "What do you take me for?"

"Some fellows would, to set Aunt Hamilton against me."

"I am not so mean as that."

"I am glad I can depend on you. You see, the old lady is awfully rich - doesn't know what to do with her money - and as she has no son, or anybody nearer than me and mother, it's natural we should inherit her money."

"I hope she will enjoy it herself for a good many years."

"Oh, she's getting old," said Conrad carelessly. "She can't expect to live forever. It wouldn't be fair for young people if their parents lived to a hundred. Now, would it?"

"I should be very glad to have my mother live to a hundred, if she could enjoy life," said Ben, disgusted with his companoin's sordid selfishness.

"Your mother hasn't got any money, and that makes a difference."

Ben had a reply, but he reflected it would be of little use to argue with one who took such widely different views as Conrad. Moreover, they were already within a block or two of the theater.

The best seats were priced at a dollar and a half, and Mrs. Hamilton had given Conrad three dollars to purchase one for Ben and one for himself.

"It seems an awful price to pay a dollar and a half for a seat," said Conrad. "Suppose we go into the gallery, where the seats are only fifty cents?"

"I think Mrs. Hamilton meant us to take higher-priced seats."

"She won't care, or know, unless we choose to tell her."

"Then you don't propose to give her back the difference?"

"You don't take me for a fool, do you? I'll tell you what I'll do. If you don't mind a fifty-cent seat, I'll give you twenty-five cents out of this money."

Ben could hardly believe Conrad was in earnest in this exhibition of meanness.

"Then," said he, "you would clear seventy-five cents on my seat and a dollar on your own?"

"You can see almost as well in the gallery," said Conrad. "I'll give you fifty cents, if you insist upon it."

"I insist upon having my share of the money spent for a seat," said Ben, contemptuously. "You can sit where you please, of course."

"You ain't very obliging," said Conrad sullenly. "I need the money, and that's what made me propose it. As you've made so much fuss about it, we'll take orchestra seats."

This he did, though unwillingly.

"I don't think I shall ever like that boy," thought Ben. "He's a little too mean."

They both enjoyed the play, Ben perhaps with the most zest, for he had never before attended a city theater. At eleven o'clock the curtain fell, and they went out.

"Come, Ben," said Conrad, "you might treat a fellow to soda water."

"I will," answered Ben. "Where shall we go?"

"Just opposite. They've got fine soda water across the street."

The boys drank their soda water, and started to go home.

"Suppose we go in somewhere and have a game of billiards?" suggested Conrad.

"I don't play," answered Ben.

"I'll teach you; come along," urged Conrad.

"It is getting late, and I would rather not."

"I suppose you go to roost with the chickens in the country?" sneered Conrad. You'll learn better in the city - if you stay."

"There is another reason," continued Ben. "I suppose it costs money to play billiards, and I have none to spare."

"Only twenty-five cents a game."

"It will be cheaper to go to bed."

"You won't do anything a fellow wants you to," grumbled Conrad. "You needn't be so mean, when you are getting ten dollars a week."

"I have plenty to do with my money, and I want to save up something every week."

On the whole the boys did not take to each other. They took very different views of life and duty, and there seemed to be small prospect of their becoming intimate friends.

Mrs. Hamilton had gone to bed when they returned, but Mrs. Hill was up watching for her son. She was a cold, disagreeable woman, but she was devoted to her boy.

"I am glad you have come home so soon," she said.

"I wanted to play a game of billiards, but Ben wouldn't," grumbled Conrad.

"If you had done so, I should have had to sit up later for you, Conrad."

"There was no use in sitting up for me. I ain't a baby," responded Conrad ungratefully.

"You know I can't sleep when I know you are out, Conrad."

"Then you're very foolish. Isn't she, Ben?"

"My mother would feel just so," answered Ben.

Mrs. Hill regarded him almost kindly. He had done her

a good turn in bringing her son home in good season.

"She may be a disagreeable woman," thought Ben, "but she is good to Conrad," and this made him regard the housekeeper with more favor.

CHAPTER XXII

A MYSTERIOUS LETTER

From time to time, Mrs. Hamilton sent Ben on errands to different parts of the city, chiefly to those who had been started in business with capital which she had supplied. One afternoon, he was sent to a tailor on Sixth Avenue with a note, the contents of which were unknown to him.

"You may wait for an answer," said Mrs. Hamilton.

He readily found the tailor's shop, and called for Charles Roberts, the proprietor.

The latter read the note, and said, in a business like tone:

"Come to the back part of the shop, and I will show you some goods."

Ben regarded him in surprise.

"Isn't there some mistake?" he said. "I didn't know I was to look at any goods."

"As we are to make a suit for you, I supposed you would have some choice in the matter," returned the tailor, equally surprised.

"May I look at the letter?" asked Ben.

The tailor put it into his hands.

It ran thus:

> "Mr. Roberts: You will make a suit for the bearer, from any goods he may select, and charge to the account of Helen Hamilton."

"Mrs. Hamilton did not tell me what was in the note," said Ben, smiling. "She is very kind."

Ben allowed himself to be guided by the tailor, and the result was a handsome suit, which was sent home in due time, and immediately attracted the attention of Conrad. Ben had privately thanked his patroness, but had felt under no obligation to tell Conrad.

"Seems to me you are getting extravagant!" said Conrad enviously.

"I don't know but I am," answered Ben good-naturedly.

"How much did you pay for it?"

"The price was thirty-five dollars."

"That's too much for a boy in your circumstances to pay."

"I think so myself, but I shall make it last a long time."

"I mean to make Aunt Hamilton buy me a new suit,"

grumbled Conrad.

"I have no objection, I am sure," said Ben.

"I didn't ask your permission," said Conrad rudely.

"I wonder what he would say if he knew that Mrs. Hamilton paid for my suit?" Ben said to himself. He wisely decided to keep the matter secret, as he knew that Conrad would be provoked to hear of this new proof of his relative's partiality for the boy whom he regarded as a rival.

Conrad lost no time in preferring his request to Mrs. Hamilton for a new suit.

"I bought you a suit two months since," said Mrs. Hamilton quietly. "Why do you come to me for another so soon?"

"Ben has a new suit," answered Conrad, a little confused.

"I don't know that that has anything to do with you. However, I will ask Ben when he had his last new suit."

Ben, who was present, replied:

"It was last November."

"Nearly a year since. I will take care that you are supplied with new suits as often as Ben."

Conrad retired from the presence of his relative much disgusted. He did not know, but suspected that Ben was indebted to Mrs. Hamilton for his new suit, and although this did not interfere with a liberal provision for him, he felt unwilling that anyone beside himself should bask in the favor of his rich relative. He made a discovery that troubled him about this time.

"Let me see your watch, Ben," he said one day.

Ben took out the watch and placed it in his hand.

"It's just like mine," said Conrad, after a critical examination.

"Is it?"

"Yes; don't you see? Where did you get it?"

"It was a gift," answered Ben.

"From my aunt?"

"It was given me by Mrs. Hamilton."

"She seems to be very kind to you," sneered Conrad, with a scowl.

"She is indeed!" answered Ben earnestly.

"You've played your cards well," said Conrad coarsely.

"I don't understand you," returned Ben coldly.

"I mean that, knowing her to be rich, you have done well to get on the blind side of her."

"I can't accept the compliment, if you mean it as such.

I don't think Mrs. Hamilton has any blind side, and the only way in which I intend to commend myself to her favor is to be faithful to her interests."

"Oh, you're mighty innocent; but all the same, you know how to feather your own nest."

"In a good sense, I hope I do. I don't suppose anyone else will take the trouble to feather it for me. I think honesty and fidelity are good policy, don't you?"

"I don't pretend to be an angel," answered Conrad sullenly.

"Nor I," said Ben, laughing.

Some days later, Conrad came to Ben one day, looking more cordial than usual.

"Ben," he said, "I have a favor to ask of you."

"What is it?"

"Will you grant it?"

"I want to know first what it is."

"Lend me five dollars?"

Ben stared at Conrad in surprise. He had just that amount, after sending home money to his mother, but he intended that afternoon to deposit three dollars of it in the savings bank, feeling that he ought to be laying up money while he was so favorably situated.

"How do you happen to be short of money?" he asked.

"That doesn't need telling. I have only four dollars a week pocket money, and I am pinched all the time."

"Then, supposing I lent you the money, how could you manage to pay me back out of this small allowance?"

"Oh, I expect to get some money in another way, but I cannot unless you lend me the money."

"Would you mind telling me how?"

"Why, the fact is, a fellow I know - that is, I have heard of him - has just drawn a prize of a thousand dollars in a Havana lottery. All he paid for his ticket was five dollars."

"And is this the way you expect to make some money?"

"Yes; I am almost sure of winning."

"Suppose you don't?"

"Oh, what's the use of looking at the dark side?"

"You are not so sensible as I thought, Conrad," said Ben. "At least a hundred draw a blank to one who draws a small prize, and the chances are a hundred to one against you."

"Then you won't lend me the money?" said Conrad angrily.

"I would rather not."

"Then you're a mean fellow!"

"Thank you for your good opinion, but I won't change my determination."

"You get ten dollars a week?"

"I shall not spend two dollars a week on my own amusement, or for my own purposes."

"What are you going to do with the rest, then?"

"Part I shall send to my mother; part I mean to put in some savings bank."

"You mean to be a miser, then?"

"If to save money makes one a miser, then I shall be one."

Conrad left the room in an angry mood. He was one with whom prosperity didn't agree. Whatever his allowance might be, he wished to spend more. Looking upon himself as Mrs. Hamilton's heir, he could not understand the need or expediency of saving money. He was not wholly to blame for this, as his mother encouraged him in hopes which had no basis except in his own and her wishes.

Not quite three weeks after Ben had become established his new home he received a letter which mystified and excited him.

It ran thus:

"If you will come at nine o'clock this evening to No. - West Thirty-first Street, and call for me, you will hear something to your advantage.

James Barnes."

"It may be something relating to my father's affairs," thought Ben. "I will go."

CHAPTER XXIII

BEN'S VISIT TO THIRTY-FIRST STREET

Ben's evenings being unoccupied, he had no difficulty in meeting the appointment made for him. He was afraid Conrad might ask him to accompany him somewhere, and thus involve the necessity of an explanation, which he did not care to give until he had himself found out why he had been summoned.

The address given by James Barnes was easy to find. Ben found himself standing before a brick building of no uncommon exterior. The second floor seemed to be lighted up; the windows were hung with crimson curtains, which quite shut out a view of what was transpiring within.

Ben rang the bell. The door was opened by a colored servant, who looked at the boy inquiringly.

"Is Mr. Barnes within?" asked Ben.

"I don't know the gentleman," was the answer.

"He sent me a letter, asking me to meet him here at nine o'clock."

"Then I guess it's all right. Are you a telegraph boy?"

"No," answered Ben, in surprise.

"I reckon it's all right," said the negro, rather to himself than to Ben. "Come upstairs."

Ben followed his guide, and at the first landing a door was thrown open. Mechanically, Ben followed the servant into the room, but he had not made half a dozen steps when he looked around in surprise and bewilderment. Novice as he was, a glance satisfied him that he was in a gambling house. The double room was covered with a soft, thick carpet, chandeliers depended from the ceiling, frequent mirrors reflecting the brilliant lights enlarged the apparent size the apartment, and a showy bar at one end of the room held forth an alluring invitation which most failed to resist. Around tables were congregated men, young and old, each with an intent look, watching the varying chances of fortune.

"I'll inquire if Mr. Barnes is here," said Peter, the colored servant.

Ben stood uneasily looking at the scene till Peter came back.

"Must be some mistake," he said. "There's no gentleman of the name of Barnes here."

"It's strange," said Ben, perplexed.

He turned to go out, but was interrupted. A man with a sinister expression, and the muscle of a prize fighter, walked up to him and said, with a scowl:

"What brings you here, kid?"

"I received a letter from Mr. Barnes, appointing to meet me here."

"I believe you are lying. No such man comes here."

"I never lie," exclaimed Ben indignantly.

"Have you got that letter about you?" asked the man suspiciously.

Ben felt in his pocket for the letter, but felt in vain.

"I think I must have left it at home," he said nervously.

The man's face darkened.

"I believe you come here as a spy," he said.

"Then you are mistaken!" said Ben, looking him fearlessly in the face.

"I hope so, for your sake. Do you know what kind of a place this is?"

"I suppose it is a gambling house," Ben answered, without hesitation.

"Did you know this before you came here?"

"I had not the least idea of it."

The man regarded him suspiciously, but no one could look into Ben's honest face and doubt his word.

"At any rate, you've found it out. Do you mean to blab?"

"No; that is no business of mine."

"Then you can go, but take care that you never come here again."

"I certainly never will."

"Give me your name and address."

"Why do you want it?"

"Because if you break your word, you will be tracked and punished."

"I have no fear," answered Ben, and he gave his name and address.

"Never admit this boy again, Peter," said the man with whom Ben had been conversing; neither this boy, nor any other, except a telegraph boy."

"All right, sah."

A minute later, Ben found himself on the street, very much perplexed by the events of the evening. Who could have invited him to a gambling house, and with what object in view? Moreover, why had not James Barnes kept the appointment he had himself made? These were questions which Ben might have been better able to answer if he could have seen, just around the corner, the triumphant look of one who was stealthily watching him.

This person was Conrad Hill, who took care to vacate his position before Ben had reached the place where he was standing.

"So far, so good!" he muttered to himself. "Master Ben has been seen coming out of a gambling house. That won't be likely to recommend him to Mrs. Hamilton, and she shall know it before long."

Ben could not understand what had become of the note summoning him to the gambling house. In fact, he had dislodged it from the vest pocket in which he thrust it, and it had fallen upon the carpet near the desk in what Mrs. Hamilton called her "office." Having occasion to enter the room in the evening, his patroness saw it on the carpet, picked it up, and read it, not without surprise.

"This is a strange note for Ben to receive," she said to herself. "I wonder what it means?"

Of course, she had no idea of the character of the place indicated, but was inclined to hope that some good luck was really in store for her young secretary.

"He will be likely to tell me sooner or later," she said to herself. "I will wait patiently, and let him choose his own time. Meanwhile I will keep the note."

Mrs. Hamilton did not see Ben till the next morning. Then he looked thoughtful, but said nothing. He was puzzling himself over what had happened. He hardly knew whether to conclude that the whole thing was a trick, or that the note was written in good faith.

"I don't understand why the writer should have appointed to meet me at such a place," he reflected. "I may hear from him again."

It was this reflection which led him to keep the matter

secret from Mrs. Hamilton, to whom be had been tempted to speak.

"I will wait till I know more," he said to himself. "This Barnes knows my address, and he can communicate with me if he chooses."

Of course, the reader understands that Conrad was at the bottom of the trick, and that the object was to persuade Mrs. Hamilton that the boy she trusted was in the habit of visiting gambling houses. The plan had been suggested by Conrad, and the details agreed on by him and his mother. This explains why Conrad was so conveniently near at hand to see Ben coming out of the gambling house.

The boy reported the success of this plan to his mother.

"I never saw a boy look so puzzled," he said, with a chuckle, "when he came out of the gambling house. I should like to know what sort of time he had there. I expected he would get kicked out."

"I feel no interest in that matter," said his mother. "I am more interested to know what Cousin Hamilton will say when she finds where her model boy has been."

"She'll give him his walking ticket, I hope."

"She ought to; but she seems so infatuated with him that there is no telling."

"When shall you tell her, mother?"

Horatio Alger, Jr.

"I will wait a day or two. I want to manage matters so as not to arouse any suspicion."

CHAPTER XXIV

BEN ON TRIAL

"Excuse my intrusion, Cousin Hamilton; I see you are engaged."

The speaker was Mrs. Hill, and the person addressed was her wealthy cousin. It was two days after the event recorded in the last chapter.

"I am only writing a note, about which there is no haste. Did you wish to speak to me?"

Mrs. Hamilton leaned back in her chair, and waited to hear what Mrs. Hill had to say. There was very little similarity between the two ladies. One was stout, with a pleasant, benevolent face, to whom not only children, but older people, were irresistibly attracted. The other was thin, with cold, gray eyes, a pursed-up mouth, thin lips, who had never succeeded in winning the affection of anyone. True, she had married, but her husband was attracted by a small sum of money which she possessed, and which had been reported to him as much larger than it really was.

When asked if she wished to speak, Mrs. Hill coughed.

"There's a matter I think I ought to speak of," she said,

Horatio Alger, Jr.

"but it is painful for me to do so."

"Why is it painful?" asked Mrs. Hamilton, eyeing her steadily.

"Because my motives may be misconstrued. Then, I fear it will give you pain."

"Pain is sometimes salutary. Has Conrad displeased you?"

"No, indeed!" answered Mrs. Hill, half indignantly. "My boy is a great comfort to me."

"I am glad to hear it," said Mrs. Hamilton dryly.

For her own part, Mrs. Hamilton thought her cousin's son one of the least attractive young people she had ever met, and save for a feeling of pity, and the slight claims of relationship, would not have been willing to keep him in the house.

"I don't see why you should have judged so ill of my poor Conrad," complained Mrs. Hill.

"I am glad you are so well pleased with him. Let me know what you have to communicate."

"It is something about the new boy - Benjamin."

Mrs. Hamilton lifted her eyebrows slightly.

"Speak without hesitation," she said.

"You will be sure not to misjudge me?"

"Why should I?"

"You might think I was jealous on account of my own boy."

"There is no occasion for you to be jealous."

"No, of course not. I am sure Conrad and I have abundant cause to be grateful to you."

"That is not telling me what you came to tell," said Mrs. Hamilton impatiently.

"I am afraid you are deceived in the boy, Cousin Hamilton."

"In what respect?"

"I am almost sorry I had not kept the matter secret. If I did not consider it my duty to you, I would have done so."

"Be kind enough to speak at once. You need not apologize, nor hesitate on my account. What has Ben been doing?"

"On Tuesday evening he was seen coming out of a well-known gambling house."

"Who saw him?"

"Conrad."

"How did Conrad know that it was a gambling house?"

"He had had it pointed out to him as such," Mrs. Hill

answered, with some hesitation.

"About what time was this?"

"A little after nine in the evening."

"And where was the gambling house situated?"

"On Thirty-first Street."

A peculiar look came over Mrs. Hamilton's face.

"And Conrad reported this to you?"

"The same evening."

"That was Tuesday?"

"Yes; I could not make up my mind to tell you immediately, because I did not want to injure the boy."

"You are more considerate than I should have expected."

"I hope I am. I don't pretend to like the boy. He seems to have something sly and underhand about him. Still, he needs to be employed, and that made me pause."

"Till your sense of duty to me overcame your reluctance?"

"Exactly so, Cousin Hamilton. I am glad you understand so well how I feel about the matter."

Mrs. Hill was quite incapable of understanding the irony of her cousin's last remark, and was inclined to be well pleased with the reception her news had met with.

"Where is Conrad?"

"He is not in the house. He didn't want me to tell you."

"That speaks well for him. I must speak to Ben on the subject."

She rang the bell, and a servant appeared.

"See if Master Ben is in his room," said the lady. "If so ask him to come here for five minutes."

Ben was in the house and in less than two minutes he entered the room. He glanced from one lady to the other in some surprise. Mrs. Hamilton wore her ordinary manner, but Mrs. Hill's mouth was more pursed up than ever. She looked straight before her, and did not look at Ben at all.

"Ben," said Mrs. Hamilton, coming to the point at once, "did you visit a gambling house in Thirty-first Street on Tuesday evening?"

"I did," answered Ben promptly.

Mrs. Hill moved her hands slightly, and looked horror-stricken.

"You must have had some good reason for doing so. I take it for granted you did not go there to gamble?"

"No," answered Ben, with a smile. "That is not in my line."

"What other purpose could he have had, Cousin Hamilton?" put in Mrs. Hill maliciously.

Ben eyed her curiously.

"Did Mrs. Hill tell you I went there?" he asked.

"I felt it my duty to do so," said that lady, with acerbity. "I dislike to see my cousin so deceived and imposed upon by one she had befriended."

"How did you know I went there, Mrs. Hill?"

"Conrad saw you coming out of the gambling house."

"I didn't see him. It was curious he happened be in that neighborhood just at that time," said Ben significantly.

"If you mean to insinuate that Conrad goes to such places, you are quite mistaken," said Mrs. Hill sharply.

"It was not that I meant to insinuate at all."

"You have not yet told me why you went there, Ben?" said Mrs. Hamilton mildly."

"Because I received a mysterious letter, signed James Barnes, asking me to come to that address about nine o'clock in the evening. I was told I would hear something of advantage to myself."

"Did you meet any such man there?" asked Mrs. Hill.

"No."

"Have you got the letter you speak of?" asked

Mrs. Hamilton.

"No," answered Ben. "I must have dropped it somewhere. I felt in my pocket for it when I reached the gambling house, but it was gone."

Mrs. Hill looked fairly triumphant.

"A very queer story!" she said, nodding her head. "I don't believe you received any such letter. I presume you had often been to the same place to misspend your evenings."

"Do you think so, Mrs. Hamilton?" inquired Ben anxiously.

"It is a pity you lost that letter, Ben."

"Yes, it is," answered Ben regretfully.

"Mrs. Hill," said Mrs. Hamilton, "if you will withdraw, I would like to say a few words to Ben in private."

"Certainly, Cousin Hamilton," returned the poor cousin, with alacrity. "I think his race is about run," she said to herself, in a tone of congratulation.

CHAPTER XXV

CONRAD TAKES A BOLD STEP

"I hope, Mrs. Hamilton, you don't suspect me of frequenting gambling houses?" said Ben, after his enemy had left the room.

"No," answered Mrs. Hamilton promptly. "I think I know you too well for that."

"I did go on Tuesday evening, I admit," continued Ben. "I saw that Mrs. Hill did not believe it, but it's true. I wish I hadn't lost the letter inviting me there. You might think I had invented the story."

"But I don't, Ben; and, for the best of all reasons, because I found the note on the carpet, and have it in my possession now."

"Have you?" exclaimed Ben gladly.

"Here it is," said the lady, as she produced the note from the desk before her. "It is singular such a note should have been sent you," she added thoughtfully.

"I think so, too. I had no suspicion when I received it, but I think now that it was written to get to into a scrape."

"Then it must have been written by an enemy. Do you know of anyone who would feel like doing you a bad turn?"

"No," answered Ben, shaking his head.

"Do you recognize the handwriting?"

"No; it may have been written by some person I know, but I have no suspicion and no clew as to who it is."

"I think we will let the matter rest for a short time. If we say nothing about it, the guilty person may betray himself."

"You are very kind to keep your confidence in me, Mrs. Hamilton," said Ben gratefully.

"I trust you as much as ever, Ben, but I shall appear not to - for a time."

Ben looked puzzled.

"I won't explain myself," said Mrs. Hamilton, with a smile, "but I intend to treat you coolly for a time, as if you had incurred my displeasure. You need not feel sensitive, however, but may consider that I am acting."

"Then it may be as well for me to act, too," suggested Ben.

"A good suggestion! You will do well to look sober and uneasy."

"I will do my best," answered Ben brightly.

The programme was carried out. To the great delight of Mrs. Hill and Conrad, Mrs. Hamilton scarcely addressed a word to Ben at the supper table. When she did speak, it was with an abruptness and coldness quite unusual for the warm-hearted woman. Ben looked depressed, fixed his eyes on his plate, and took very little part in the conversation. Mrs. Hill and Conrad, on the other hand, seemed in very good spirits. They chatted cheerfully, and addressed an occasional word to Ben. They could afford to be magnanimous, feeling that he had forfeited their rich cousin's favor.

After supper, Conrad went into his mother's room.

"Our plan's working well, mother," he said, rubbing his hands.

"Yes, Conrad, it is. Cousin Hamilton is very angry with the boy. She scarcely spoke a word to him."

"He won't stay long, I'll be bound. Can't you suggest, mother, that he had better be dismissed at once?"

"No, Conrad; we have done all that is needed. We can trust Cousin Hamilton to deal with him. She will probably keep him for a short time, till she can get along without his services."

"It's lucky he lost the letter. Cousin Hamilton will think he never received any."

So the precious pair conferred together. It was clear that Ben had two dangerous and unscrupulous enemies in the house.

It was all very well to anticipate revenge upon Ben,

and his summary dismissal, but this did not relieve Conrad from his pecuniary embarrassments. As a general thing, his weekly allowance was spent by the middle of the week. Ben had refused to lend money, and there was no one else he could call upon. Even if our hero was dismissed, there seemed likely to be no improvement in this respect.

At this juncture, Conrad was, unfortunately, subjected to a temptation which proved too strong for him.

Mrs. Hamilton was the possessor of an elegant opera glass, which she had bought some years previous in Paris at a cost of fifty dollars. Generally, when not in use, she kept it locked up in a bureau drawer. It so happened, however, that it had been left out on a return from a matinee, and lay upon her desk, where it attracted the attention of Conrad.

It was an unlucky moment, for he felt very hard up. He wished to go to the theater in the evening with a friend, but had no money.

It flashed upon him that he could raise a considerable sum on the opera glass at Simpson's, a well-known pawnbroker on the Bowery, and he could, without much loss of time, stop there on his way down to business.

Scarcely giving himself time to think, he seized the glass and thrust it into the pocket of his overcoat. Then, putting on his coat, he hurried from the house.

Arrived at the pawnbroker's, he produced the glass, and asked:

"How much will you give me on this?"

The attendant looked at the glass, and then at Conrad.

"This is a very valuable glass," he said. "Is it yours?"

"No," answered Conrad glibly. "It belongs to a lady in reduced circumstances, who needs to raise money. She will be able to redeem it soon."

"Did she send you here?"

"Yes."

"We will loan you twenty dollars on it. Will that be satisfactory?"

"Quite so," answered Conrad, quite elated at the sum, which exceeded his anticipations.

"Shall we make out the ticket to you or the lady?"

"To me. The lady does not like to have her name appear in the matter."

This is so frequently the case that the statement created no surprise.

"What is your name?" inquired the attendant.

"Ben Barclay," answered Conrad readily.

The ticket was made out, the money paid over, and Conrad left the establishment.

"Now I am in funds!" he said to himself, "and there is

no danger of detection. If anything is ever found out, it will be Ben who will be in trouble, not I."

It was not long before Mrs. Hamilton discovered her loss. She valued the missing opera glass, for reasons which need not be mentioned, far beyond its intrinsic value, and though she could readily have supplied its place, so far as money was concerned, she would not have been as well pleased with any new glass, though precisely similar, as with the one she had used for years. She remembered that she had not replaced the glass in the drawer, and, therefore, searched for it wherever she thought it likely to have been left. But in vain.

"Ben," she said, "have you seen my glass anywhere about?"

"I think," answered Ben, "that I saw it on your desk."

"It is not there now, but it must be somewhere in the house."

She next asked Mrs. Hill. The housekeeper was entirely ignorant of Conrad's theft, and answered that she had not seen it.

"I ought not to have left it about," said Mrs. Hamilton. "It may have proved too strong a temptation to some one of the servants."

"Or someone else," suggested Mrs. Hill significantly.

"That means Ben," thought Mrs. Hamilton, but she did not say so.

"I would ferret out the matter if I were you," continued Mrs. Hill.

"I intend to," answered Mrs. Hamilton quietly. "I valued the glass far beyond its cost, and I will leave no means untried to recover it."

"You are quite right, too."

When Conrad was told that the opera glass had been lost, he said:

"Probably Ben stole it."

"So I think," assented his mother. "But it will be found out. Cousin Hamilton has put the matter into the hands of a detective."

For the moment, Conrad felt disturbed. But he quickly recovered himself.

"Pshaw! they can't trace it to me," he thought. "They will put it on Ben."

CHAPTER XXVI

MR. LYNX, THE DETECTIVE

The detective who presented himself to Mrs. Hamilton was a quiet-looking man, clad in a brown suit. Except that his eyes were keen and searching, his appearance was disappointing. Conrad met him as he was going out of the house, and said to himself contemptuously: "He looks like a muff."

"I have sent for you, Mr. Lynx," said Mrs. Hamilton, "to see if you can help me in a matter I will explain to you," and then she gave him all the information she possessed about the loss of the opera glass.

"How valuable was the glass?" inquired Mr. Lynx.

"It cost fifty dollars in Paris," said Mrs. Hamilton.

"But you set a higher value upon it for other reasons? Just so."

"You are right."

"Will you favor me with an exact description of the article?" said the detective, producing his notebook.

Mrs. Hamilton did so, and the detective made an entry.

Horatio Alger, Jr.

"Have you ever had anything taken out of your house by outside parties?" he asked.

"On one occasion, when my brother was visiting me, his overcoat was taken from the hatstand in the hall."

"A sneak thief, of course. The glass, however, was not so exposed?"

"No; it was not on the lower floor at all."

"It looks, then, as if it was taken by someone in the house."

"It looks so," said Mrs. Hamilton gravely.

"Have you confidence in your servants? Or, rather, have you reason to suspect any of them?"

"I believe they are honest. I don't believe they would be tempted by such an article."

"Not, perhaps, for their own use, but a glass like this may be pawned for a considerable sum. Being of peculiar appearance, the thief would be hardly likely to use it himself or herself. Detection would be too sure."

"No doubt you are right."

"How long has the glass been missing?" resumed the detective.

"Three days."

"No doubt it has been pawned by this time. Your course is clear."

"And what is that?"

"To make a tour of the pawnshops, and ascertain whether such an article has been brought to any one of them."

"Very well, Mr. Lynx. I leave the matter in your hands. I trust everything to your judgment."

"Thank you. I will try to deserve your confidence. And now, good-day. I may call upon you to-morrow."

"Mr. Lynx left the presence of the lady, and went downstairs. He had just reached the bottom of the staircase, when a thin lady glided from the rear of the hall, and spoke to him.

"Are you the detective summoned by Mrs. Hamilton?" she asked.

"Yes, madam," answered Mr. Lynx, surveying house-keeper attentively.

"I am Mrs. Hill, the housekeper," said she. "I may add that I am a cousin of Mrs. Hamilton's."

Mr. Lynx bowed, and waited for further information. He knew who was addressing him, for he had questioned Mrs. Hamilton as to the different inmates of the house.

"I stopped you," said Mrs. Hill, "because I have my suspicions, and I thought I might help you in this investigation."

"I shall feel indebted to you for any help you can

Horatio Alger, Jr.

afford. Do you mind telling me upon what your suspicions rest?"

"I don't like to accuse or throw suspicions on anyone," said the housekeeper, but I think it is my duty to help my cousin in this matter."

"Undoubtedly," said Mr. Lynx, noticing that she paused. "Proceed."

"You may or may not be aware that my cousin employs a boy of about sixteen, whom, as I think, she engaged rather rashly, without knowing anything of his antecedents. He assists her in her writing and accounts - in fact, is a sort of secretary.

"His name is Benjamin Barclay, is it not?"

"Yes."

"Do you know anything of his habits?"

"He is very plausible. In fact, I think his appearance is in his favor; but I think he is sly. Still water, you know, runs deep."

Mr. Lynx bowed assent.

"I was disposed," proceeded Mrs. Hill artfully, "to think well of the boy, and to approve my cousin's selection, until last week he was seen leaving a well-known gambling house in Thirty-first Street."

"Indeed! That is certainly suspicious."

"Is it not?"

"Who saw him leaving the gambling house, Mrs. Hill?"

"My son, Conrad."

"Curious that he should have been near at the time!"

"He was taking a walk. He generally goes out in the evening."

"Of course your son would not visit such a place?"

"Certainly not," answered Mrs. Hill, looking offended at the suggestion.

"By the way, are the two boys intimate? Do they seem to like each other?"

"My Conrad always treats the other boy well, out of common politeness, but I don't think he likes him very well."

"Is your son in any situation?"

"He is now."

"Was he at the time this Benjamin was engaged by Mrs. Hamilton?"

"No."

"Rather singular that she did not employ your son, instead of seeking out a stranger, isn't it?"

"Now that you mention it, I confess that I did feel hurt at the slight to my boy. However, I don't wish to interfere with Cousin Hamilton, or obtrude my son upon her."

"Strong jealousy there!" thought the detective.

"So you think this Ben Barclay may have taken the glass?" he said inquiringly.

"I do. Since he visits gambling houses, he doubtless squanders money, and can find a market for more than he can honestly earn."

"As you say, gambling often leads to dishonesty. Does Mrs. Hamilton know that her protege visited a gambling house?"

"Yes."

"Mentioned it to him, I suppose?"

"Yes."

"Of course, he denied it?"

"No; he admitted it, but said he received a letter from a stranger appointing to meet him there. It is rather curious that he couldn't show the letter, however. He pretended he had lost it."

"Did Mrs. Hamilton believe him?"

"I don't know. I think not, for, though she has not discharged him, she treats him very coldly."

"Have you any further information to give me?"

"No. I hope this will be of some service to you."

"I think it will. Thank you, and good-afternoon."

"There! I've prejudiced him against Ben," said Mrs. Hill to herself, with a satisfied smile. "These detectives are glad of a hint, sharp as they think themselves. If he finds out that it is Ben, he will take all the credit to himself, and never mention me in the matter. However, that is just what I wish. It is important that I should not appear too active in getting the boy into trouble, or I may be thought to be influenced by interested motives, though, Heaven knows, I only want justice for myself and my boy. The sooner we get this boy out of the house, the better it will be for us."

As Mr. Lynx left the house, he smiled to himself.

"That woman and her son hate Ben Barclay, that much is certain, and look upon him as an interloper and a rival. I rather sympathize with the poor fellow. I should be sorry to find him guilty, but I shall not stop short till I have ferreted out the truth."

CHAPTER XXVII

THE TELLTALE TICKET

Conrad still had the pawnbroker's ticket which he had received in return for the opera glasses, and did not quite know what to do with it. He didn't intend to redeem the glass, and if found in his possession, it would bring him under suspicion. Now that a detective had the matter in charge, it occurred to him that it would be well to have the ticket found in Ben's room.

The two had rooms upon the same floor, and it would, therefore, be easy to slip into Ben's chamber and leave it somewhere about.

Now, it chanced that Susan, the chambermaid, was about, though Conrad did not see her, when he carried out his purpose, and, instigated by curiosity, she peeped through the half-open door, and saw him place the ticket on the bureau.

Wondering what it was, she entered the room after Conrad had vacated it, and found the ticket Conrad had placed there.

Susan knew what a pawnbroker's ticket was, and read it with curiosity.

She saw that it was made out to Ben Barclay.

"How, then, did Master Conrad get hold of it?" she said to herself. "It's my belief he's trying to get Master Ben into trouble. It's a shame, it is, for Master Ben is a gentleman and he isn't."

Between the two boys, Susan favored Ben, who always treated her with consideration, while Conrad liked to order about the servants, as if they were made to wait upon him.

After Conrad had disposed of the pawn ticket, he said carelessly to his mother:

"Mother, if I were you, I'd look into Ben's room. You might find the opera glass there."

"I don't think he'd leave it there. He would pawn it."

"Then you might find the ticket somewhere about."

Upon this hint, Mrs. Hill went up to Ben's room, and there, upon the bureau, she naturally found the ticket.

"I thought so," she said to herself. "Conrad was right. The boy is a thief. Here is the ticket made out to him by name. Well, well, he's brazen enough, in all conscience. Now shall I show it to Cousin Hamilton at once, or shall I wait until the detective has reported?"

On the whole, Mrs. Hill decided to wait. She could delay with safety, for she had proof which would utterly crush and confound the hated interloper.

Meanwhile, the detective pursued his investigations.

Of course, he visited Simpson's, and there he learned that the opera glass, which he readily recognized from the description, had been brought there a few days previous.

"Who brought it?" he asked.

"A boy of about sixteen."

"Did he give his name?"

The books were referred to, and the attendant answered in the affirmative.

"He gave the name of Ben Barclay," he answered.

"Do you think that was his real name?" asked the detective.

"That depends on whether he had a right to pawn it."

"Suppose he stole it?"

"Then, probably, he did not give his real name."

"So I think," said Mr. Lynx quietly.

"Do you know if there is a boy by that name?"

"There is; but I doubt if he knows anything about the matter."

"I will call again, perhaps to-morrow," he added. "I must report to my principal what I have discovered."

From Simpson's he went straight to Mrs. Hamilton,

who had as yet received no communication from the housekeeper.

"Well, Mr. Lynx," she asked, with interest, "have you heard anything of the glass?"

"I have seen it," was the quiet reply.

"Where?"

"At a well-known pawnshop on the Bowery."

"Did you learn who left it?" asked Mrs. Hamilton eagerly.

"A boy - about sixteen years of age - who gave the name of Ben Barclay."

"I can't believe Ben would be guilty of such a disgraceful act!" ejaculated Mrs. Hamilton, deeply moved.

CHAPTER XXVIII

MRS. HILL'S MALICE

At this moment there was a low knock on the door.

"Come in!" said Mrs. Hamilton.

Mrs. Hill, the housekeeper, glided in, with her usual stealthy step.

"I really beg pardon for intruding," she said, with a slight cough, "but I thought perhaps I might throw light on the matter Mr. Lynx is investigating."

"Well?" said the detective, eying her attentively.

"I had occasion to go into Ben's room to see if the girl had put things in order, when my attention was drawn to a ticket upon the bureau. You can tell whether it is of importance," and she handed it, with an air of deference, to Mr. Lynx.

"What is it?" asked Mrs. Hamilton.

"It is a pawn ticket," answered Mr. Lynx attentively.

"Let me see it, please!"

Mrs. Hamilton regarded it with mingled pain and incredulity.

"I need not say," continued the housekeeper, "that I was surprised and saddened at this evidence of the boy's depravity. Cousin Hamilton has been so kind to him that it seems like the height of ingratitude."

"May I ask, madam," said Mr. Lynx, "if your suspicions had fastened on this boy, Ben, before you found the pawn ticket?"

"To tell the truth, they had."

"And what reason had you for forming such suspicions?"

"I knew that the boy frequented gambling houses, and, of course, no salary, however large, would be sufficient for a boy with such habits."

Mrs. Hamilton did not speak, which somewhat embarrassed Mrs. Hill. Mr. Lynx, however, was very affable, and thanked her for her assistance.

"I felt it my duty to assist Cousin Hamilton," said she, "though I am sorry for that ungrateful boy. I will now withdraw, and leave you to confer together."

Mrs. Hill would like to have been invited to remain, but such an invitation was not given.

"What do you think, Mr. Lynx?" asked Mrs. Hamilton.

"I think your housekeeper does not like Ben Barclay," he answered dryly.

Horatio Alger, Jr.

"And you don't think him guilty?" she asked eagerly.

"No; the boy isn't fool enough, first, to give his own name at the pawnbroker's, and next, to leave the ticket exposed in his room."

"How then did it come there?"

Mr. Lynx was saved the trouble of answering by another tap on the door.

"Who is it now?" he said.

He stepped to the door, and opening it, admitted Susan.

"What is it, Susan," asked Mrs. Hamilton, in some surprise.

"Did Mrs. Hill bring you a pawn ticket, ma'am?"

"And what do you know about it?" demanded Mr. Lynx brusquely.

"And did she say she found it on Master Ben's bureau?"

"Yes, Susan," said the mistress; "what can you tell us about it?"

"I can tell you this, ma'am, that I saw Master Conrad steal into the room this morning, and put it there with his own hands."

"Ha! this is something to the purpose." said the detective briskly.

"Are you sure of this, Susan?" asked Mrs. Hamilton, evidently shocked.

"I can take my Bible oath of it, ma'am; and it's my belief that he's tryin' to get Master Ben into trouble."

"Thank you, Susan," said her mistress. "You have done not only Ben, but myself, a valuable service. You can go. I will see that you do not regret it."

"Don't tell Mrs. Hill that I told you, or she'd be my enemy for life!"

"I will see to that."

As Susan left the room, Mr. Lynx said:

"You won't require my services any longer. It is clear enough who pawned the glass."

"You mean - "

"I mean the boy Conrad, whose mother was so anxious to fix the guilt upon your young secretary. If you have the slightest doubt about it, invite the young gentleman to accompany you to Simpson's to redeem the opera glass."

"I will."

CHAPTER XXIX

SOME UNEXPECTED CHANGES

When Conrad came home his first visit was to his mother.

"Has anything been found out about the stolen opera glass?" he asked, with a studied air of indifference.

"I should say there had," she answered. "I followed the clew you suggested, and searched the boy's room. On the bureau I found the pawn ticket."

"You don't say so! What a muff Ben must have been to leave it around so carelessly! What did you do with it?"

"I waited till Mr. Lynx was conferring with Cousin Hamilton, and then I carried it in and gave it to them."

"What did they say?" asked Conrad eagerly.

"They seemed thunderstruck, and Mr. Lynx very politely thanked me for the help I had given them."

"Has Ben been bounced yet?"

"No; but doubtless he will be very soon. Cousin

Hamilton doesn't want to think him a thief and gambler, but there seems no way of escaping from such a mass of proof."

"I should say not. Do you think she's told Ben? Does he look down in the mouth?" continued Conrad.

"I haven't seen him since."

When they met at the table Mrs. Hamilton's manner toward Ben was decidedly frigid, as Conrad and his mother saw, much to their satisfaction. Ben looked sober, but his appetite did not appear to be affected.

"Your course is about run, young man!" thought Mrs. Hill.

"I should like to see you after supper, Conrad," said Mrs. Hamilton. "Come into my sitting room."

"I wonder if she is going to give me Ben's place," thought Conrad, hardly knowing whether he wished it or not.

With a jaunty air and a self-satisfied smile, he followed Mrs. Hamilton into her "private office," as she sometimes called it.

"Shut the door, Conrad," she said.

He did so.

"I have heard news of the opera glass," she commenced.

"Mother gave me a hint of that," said Conrad.

"It was stolen and pawned at Simpson's on the Bowery."

"It's a great shame!" said Conrad, thinking that a safe comment to make.

"Yes, it was a shame and a disgrace to the one who took it."

"I didn't think Ben would do such a thing," continued Conrad, growing bolder.

"Nor I," said Mrs. Hamilton.

"After all you have done for him, too. I never liked the boy, for my part."

"So I suspected," said Mrs. Hamilton dryly. "However, I will tell you what I want of you. I am going down to Simpson's to-morrow to redeem the glass, and want you to go with me."

"You want me to go with you!" ejaculated Conrad, turning pale.

"Yes; I don't care to go to that part of the City by myself, and I will take you to keep me company."

"But I must go to the office," faltered Conrad.

"I will send Ben to say that you can't go to-morrow."

"Why don't you take Ben to Simpson's, or the detective?" suggested Conrad, in great alarm, bethinking himself that it would hardly do to take Ben, since the attendant would certify that he was not the one who pawned the glass.

"Because I prefer to take you. Have you any objection to go!"

"Oh, no, of course not!" answered Conrad, not daring to make any further objection.

In the morning Mrs. Hill came to Mrs. Hamilton, and said:

"Poor Conrad has a terrible toothache! He is afraid he won't be able to go with you to Simpson's. Will you kindly excuse him?"

Mrs. Hamilton expected some such excuse.

"I will take Ben, then," she said.

"Are you going to keep that boy - after what be has done?" asked the housekeeper.

"It is inconvenient for me to part with him just yet."

"Then - I hope you will excuse the suggestion - I advise you to keep your bureau drawers locked."

"I think it best myself," said Mrs. Hamilton. Is Conrad's toothache very bad?"

"The poor fellow is in great pain."

When Ben was invited by Mrs. Hamilton to go to the pawnbroker's he made no objection.

"It is only fair to tell you, Ben," said Mrs. Hamilton,

Horatio Alger, Jr.

that the person who pawned the opera glass gave your name."

"Then," said Ben, "I should like to know who it is."

"I think I know," said his patroness; "but when we redeem the glass we will ask for a description of him."

An hour later they entered the pawnbroker's shop. Mrs. Hamilton presented the ticket and made herself known.

"Will you tell me," she asked, "whether you have ever seen the young gentleman that accompanies me?"

"Not to my knowledge," answered the attendant, after attentively regarding Ben.

"Can you remember the appearance of the boy who pawned the opera glass?"

"He was taller than this boy, and pale. He was thinner also. His hair was a light brown."

A light dawned upon Ben, and his glance met that of Mrs. Hamilton, so that she read his suspicions.

"I think we both know who it was that took your name, Ben," she said; "but for the present I wish you to keep it secret."

"I will certainly do so, Mrs. Hamilton."

"I am placed in difficult circumstances, and have not made up my mind what to do."

"I hope you won't allow yourself to be prejudiced

against me by any false stories."

"No, I can promise you that. I have perfect confidence in you."

"Thank you for that, Mrs. Hamilton," said Ben gratefully.

"Yet I am about to take a course that will surprise you."

"What is that?"

"I am going to let you leave me for a time, and put Conrad in your place."

Ben looked bewildered, as well he might. There was nothing that would have surprised him more.

"Then I am afraid you don't find me satisfactory," he said anxiously.

"Why not?"

"You discharge me from your service."

"No" answered Mrs. Hamilton, smiling; "I have other work for you to do. I mean to give you a confidential commission."

Ben's face brightened up immediately.

"You will find me faithful," he said, "and I hope I may repay your confidence."

"I think you will. I will explain matters to you before

you reach the house, as I don't want Mrs. Hill or Conrad to know about the matter. Indeed, for reasons of my own, I shall let them think that I discharged you."

Ben smiled; he was not averse to such a plan.

"And now for the business. I own a farm in the western part of Pennsylvania. I have for years let it for a nominal sum to a man named Jackson. Of late he has been very anxious to buy it, and has offered me a sum greater than I had supposed it to be worth. As I know him to be a close-fisted man, who has tried more than once to get me to reduce the small rent I charge him, this naturally excites my curiosity. I think something has been discovered that enhances the value of the farm, and, if so, I want to know it. You are a boy, and a visit to the neighborhood will not excite surprise.

"I understand," said Ben. "When do you wish me to start?"

"This afternoon. I have prepared written instructions, and here is a pocketbook containing a hundred and fifty dollars for expenses."

"Shall I need so much?"

"Probably not; but I wish you to be amply provided. You will remove all your things from my house, but you may store anything you don't need to carry."

When Conrad heard that Mrs. Hamilton had taken Ben with her, he was alarmed lest it should be discovered that the boy pawning the opera glass was not Ben, but himself. When, upon Mrs. Hamilton's return, he was summoned to her presence, he entered with trepidation.

"Is your toothache better, Conrad?" asked Mrs. Hamilton.

"A little better, thank you."

"I am going to make a change in your position. Ben is to leave me, and you will take his place as my secretary."

Conrad's heart bounded with joy and surprise.

"How can I thank you, Cousin Hamilton!" he said, with a feeling of great relief.

"By serving me well."

"All has turned out for the best, mother," said Conrad joyfully, as he sought his mother's presence. "Ben is bounced, and I am to take his place."

"Heaven be praised!" ejaculated Mrs. Hill.

"I hope you'll soon find a place," said Conrad mockingly, when Ben left the house, valise in hand.

"I think I shall," answered Ben calmly.

Horatio Alger, Jr.

CHAPTER XXX

BEN "GOES WEST"

Undisturbed by the thought that his departure was viewed with joy by Conrad and his mother, Ben set out on his Western journey.

His destination was Centerville, in Western Pennsylvania. I may as well say that this is not the real name of the place, which, for several reasons, I conceal.

Though Ben was not an experienced traveler, he found no difficulty in reaching his destination, having purchased a copy of "Appleton's Railway Guide," which afforded him all the information he required. About fifty miles this side of Centerville he had for a seat companion a man of middle age, with a pleasant face, covered with a brown beard, who, after reading through a Philadelphia paper which he had purchased of the train-boy, seemed inclined to have a social chat with Ben.

"May I ask your destination, my young friend?" he asked.

Ben felt that it was well for him to be cautious, though he was pleasantly impressed with the appearance of his companion.

"I think I shall stop over at Centerville," he said.

"Indeed! That is my destination."

"Do you live there?" asked Ben.

"No," said the other, laughing. "Do I look like it? I thought you would read 'New York' in my face and manner."

"I am not an experienced observer," said Ben modestly.

"Centerville has a prosperous future before it," said the stranger.

"Has it? I don't know much about the place. I never was there."

"You know, of course, that it is in the oil region?"

"I didn't even know that."

"A year ago," resumed the stranger, "it was a humdrum farming town, and not a very prosperous one either. The land is not of good quality, and the farmers found it hard work to get a poor living. Now all is changed."

Ben's attention was aroused. He began to understand why Mr. Jackson wished to buy the farm he rented from Mrs. Hamilton.

"This is all new to me," he said. "I suppose oil has been found there?"

"Yes; one old farm, which would have been dear at three thousand dollars, is now yielding hundreds of barrels daily, and would fetch fifty thousand dollars easily."

Ben began to be excited. If he could only sell Mrs. Hamilton's farm for half that he felt that he would be doing an excellent thing.

"I suppose you are interested in some of the petroleum wells?" he said.

"Not yet, but I hope to be. In fact, I don't mind confessing that I represent a New York syndicate, and that my object in making this journey is to purchase, if I can, the Jackson farm."

"The Jackson farm!" repeated Ben, his breath almost taken away by his surprise.

"Yes; do you know anything about it?" asked his companion.

"I have heard of a farmer in Centerville named Peter Jackson."

"That is the man."

"And his farm is one of the lucky ones, then?"

"It promises to be."

"I suppose, then, you will have to pay a large sum for it?" said Ben, trying to speak calmly.

"Jackson is very coy, and, I think, grasping. He wants

fifty thousand dollars."

"Of course you won't pay so much?"

"I should hardly feel authorized to do so. I may go as high as forty thousand dollars."

Ben was dazzled. If he could effect a sale at this price he would be doing a splendid stroke of business, and would effectually defeat the plans of Mr. Jackson, who, it appeared, had pretended that he was the owner of the farm, hoping to obtain it from Mrs. Hamilton at a valuation which would have been suitable before the discovery of oil, but now would be ludicrously disproportionate to its real value.

"Shall or shall I not, tell this gentleman the truth?" he reflected.

He thought over the matter and decided to do so. The discovery must be made sooner or later, and there would be no advantage in delay.

"I don't think Jackson will sell," he said.

"Why not?" asked the stranger, in surprise. "Do you know him?"

"I never saw him in my life."

"Then how can you form any opinion on the subject?"

Ben smiled.

"The answer is easy enough," he said. "Mr. Jackson can't sell what he doesn't own."

"Do you mean to say that he is not the owner of the farm which he proposes to sell us?"

"That is just what I mean. He is no more the owner than you or I."

"You speak confidently, young man. Perhaps you can tell me who is the owner?"

"I can. The owner is Mrs. Hamilton, of New York."

"Indeed! That is a genuine surprise. Can you give me her address? I should like to communicate with her."

"I will cheerfully give you her address, but it won't be necessary, for I represent her."

"You!" exclaimed the stranger incredulously.

"Yes; and I am going out to Centerville now as her agent. This Jackson, who is her tenant, has been urging her to sell him the farm for some time. He has offered a sum larger than the farm would be worth but for the discovery of petroleum, but has taken good care not to speak of this."

"How much does he offer?"

"Five thousand dollars."

"The rascal!" He offers five thousand, and expects us to pay him fifty thousand dollars for his bargain. What an unmitigated swindle it would have been if he had carried out his scheme!"

"Perhaps you would like to see his last letter?"

said Ben.

"I should. I want to see what the old rascal has to say for himself."

Ben took from his pocket the letter in question, and put it into the hands of his new acquaintance.

It was dated at Centerville, October 21. It was written in a cramped hand, showing that the farmer was not accustomed to letter-writing.

It ran thus:

> "Respected Madam:
>
> "As I have already wrote you, I would like to buy the farm, and will give you more than anybody else, because I am used to living on it, and it seems like home. I am willing to pay five thousand dollars, though I know it is only worth four, but it is worth more to me than to others. I offer you more because I know you are rich, and will not sell unless you get a good bargain. Please answer right away.
>
> > "Yours respectfully,
> > Peter Jackson.
>
> "P.S. - My offer will hold good for only two weeks."

"He seems to be very much in earnest," said Ben.

"He has reason to be so, as he hopes to make forty-five thousand dollars on his investment."

"He will be bitterly disappointed," said Ben.

"I don't care anything about Jackson," said the stranger. "I would just as soon negotiate with you. Are you authorized to sell the farm?"

"No," answered Ben; "but Mrs. Hamilton will probably be guided by my advice in the mater."

"That amounts to the same thing. I offer you forty thousand dollars for it."

"I think favorably of your proposal, Mr. - "

"My name is Taylor."

"Mr. Taylor; but I prefer to delay answering till I am on the ground and can judge better of the matter."

"You are right. I was surprised at first that Mrs. Hamilton should have selected so young an agent. I begin to think her choice was a judicious one."

CHAPTER XXXI

MR. JACKSON RECEIVES A CALL

"Suppose we join forces, Ben," said Mr. Taylor familiarly.

"How do you mean?"

"We will join forces against this man Jackson. He wants to swindle both of us - that is, those whom we represent.

"I am willing to work with you" answered Ben, who had been favorably impressed by the appearance and frankness of his traveling companion.

"Then suppose to-morrow morning - it is too late to-day - we call over and see the old rascal."

"I would rather not have him know on what errand I come, just at first."

"That is in accordance with my own plans. You will go as my companion. He will take you for my son, or nephew, and, while I am negotiating, you can watch and judge for yourself."

"I like the plan," said Ben.

Horatio Alger, Jr.

"When he finds out who you are he will feel pretty badly sold."

"He deserves it."

The two put up at a country hotel, which, though not luxurious, was tolerably comfortable. After the fatigue of his journey, Ben enjoyed a good supper and a comfortable bed. The evening, however, he spent in the public room of the inn, where he had a chance to listen to the conversation of a motley crowd, some of them native and residents, others strangers who had been drawn to Centerville by the oil discoveries.

"I tell you," said a long, lank individual, "Centerville's goin' to be one of the smartest places in the United States. It's got a big future before it."

"That's so," said a small, wiry man; "but I'm not so much interested in that as I am in the question whether or not I've got a big future before me."

"You're one of the owners of the Hoffman farm, ain't you?"

"Yes. I wish I owned the whole of it. Still, I've made nigh on to a thousand dollars durin' the last month for my share of the profits. Pretty fair, eh?"

"I should say so. You've got a good purchase; but there's one better in my opinion."

"Where's that?"

"Peter Jackson's farm."

Here Ben and Mr. Taylor began to listen with interest.

"He hasn't begun to work it any, has he?"

"Not much; just enough to find out its value."

"What's he waitin' for?"

"There's some New York people want it. If he can get his price, he'll sell it to them for a good sum down."

"What does he ask?"

"He wants fifty thousand dollars."

"Whew! that's rather stiffish. I thought the property belonged to a lady in New York."

"So it did; but Jackson says he bought it a year ago."

"He was lucky."

Ben and Mr. Taylor looked at each other again. It was easy to see the old farmer's game, and to understand why he was so anxious to secure the farm, out of which he could make so large a sum of money.

"He's playing a deep game, Ben," said Taylor, when they had left the room.

"Yes; but I think I shall be able to put a spoke in his wheel."

"I shall be curious to see how he takes it when he finds the negotiation taken out of his hands. We'll play with him a little, as a cat plays with a mouse."

The next morning, after a substantial breakfast, Ben and his new friend took a walk to the farm occupied by Peter Jackson. It was about half a mile away, and when reached gave no indication of the wealth it was capable of producing. The farmhouse was a plain structure nearly forty years old, badly in need of paint, and the out-buildings harmonized with it in appearance.

A little way from the house was a tall, gaunt man, engaged in mending a fence. He was dressed in a farmer's blue frock and overalls, and his gray, stubby beard seemed to be of a week's growth. There was a crafty, greedy look in his eyes, which overlooked a nose sharp and aquiline. His feet were incased in a pair of cowhide boots. He looked inquiringly at Taylor as he approached, but hardly deigned to look at Ben, who probably seemed too insignificant to notice. He gave a shrewd guess at the errand of the visitor, but waited for him to speak first.

"Is this Mr. Jackson?" asked Taylor, with a polite bow.

"That's my name, stranger," answered the old man.

"My name is Taylor. I wrote to you last week."

"I got the letter," said Jackson, going on with his work. It was his plan not to seem too eager but to fight shy in order to get his price. Besides, though he would have been glad to close the bargain on the spot, there was an embarrassing difficulty. The farm was not his to sell, and he was anxiously awaiting Mrs. Hamilton's answer to his proposal.

"She can't have heard of the oil discoveries," he thought, "and five thousand dollars will seem a big price for the farm. She can't help agreeing to my terms."

This consideration made him hopeful, but for all that, he must wait, and waiting he found very tantalizing.

"Have you decided to accept my offer, Mr. Jackson?"

"Waal, I'll have to take a leetle time to consider. How much did you say you'd give?"

"Forty thousand dollars."

"I'd ought to have fifty."

"Forty thousand dollars is a big sum of money."

"And this farm is a perfect gold mine. Shouldn't wonder if it would net a hundred thousand dollars."

"There is no certainty of that, and the purchasers will have to take a big risk"

"There isn't much risk. Ask anybody in Centerville what he thinks of the Jackson farm."

"Suppose I were ready to come to your terms - mind, I don't say I am - would you sign the papers to-day?"

Jackson looked perplexed. He knew could not do it.

"What's your hurry?" he said.

"The capitalists whom I represent are anxious to get to work as soon as possible. That's natural, isn't, it?"

"Ye-es," answered Jackson.

"So, the sooner we fix matters the better. I want to go back to New York to-morrow if I can."

"I don't think I can give my answer as soon as that. Wait a minute, though."

A boy was approaching, Jackson's son, if one could judge from the resemblance, holding a letter in his hand.

"Come right here, Abner," he called out eagerly.

Abner approached, and his father snatched the letter from his hand. It bore the New York postmark, but, on opening it, Jackson looked bitterly disappointed. He had hoped it was from Mrs. Hamilton, accepting his offer for the farm; but, instead of that, it was an unimportant circular.

"I'll have to take time to think over your offer, Mr. Taylor," he said. "You see, I'll have to talk over matters with the old woman."

"By the way," said Taylor carelessly, "I was told in the village that you didn't own the farm - that it was owned by a lady in New York."

"She used to own it," said the fanner, uneasily; "but I bought it of her a year ago."

"So that you have the right to sell it?"

"Of course I have."

"What have you to say to that, Ben?" asked Taylor quietly.

"That if Mrs. Hamilton has sold the farm to Mr. Jackson she doesn't know it."

"What do you mean, boy?" gasped Jackson.

"I mean that when I left New York Mrs. Hamilton owned the farm."

"It's a lie!" muttered the farmer; but he spoke with difficulty. "I bought it a year ago."

"In that case it is strange that you should have written a week ago offering five thousand dollars for the farm."

"Who says I wrote?"

"I do; and I have your letter in my pocket," answered Ben firmly.

CHAPTER XXXII

BEN SELLS THE FARM

The farmer stared at Ben panic-stricken. He had thought success within his grasp. He was to be a rich man - independent for life - as the result of the trick which he was playing upon Mrs. Hamilton. His disappointment was intense, and he looked the picture of discomfiture.

"I don't believe you," he faltered after a pause.

Ben drew a letter from his inside pocket and held it up.

"Do you deny the writing?" he said.

"Give it to me!" said Jackson, with a sudden movement.

"No, thank you; I prefer to keep it. I shall make no use of it unless it is necessary. I called here to notify you that Mrs. Hamilton does not propose to sacrifice the farm. If it is sold at all it will be to someone who will pay its full value."

"You can't sell it," said Jackson sullenly. "I have a lease."

"Produce it."

"At any rate, I shall stay till my year's out."

"That will depend upon the new owner. If he is willing, Mrs. Hamilton will not object."

"I think you've got him there, Ben," said Mr. Taylor, with a laugh. "Mr. Jackson, I think it won't be worth while to continue our conversation. You undertook to sell what was not yours. I prefer to deal with the real owner or her representative."

"That boy is an impostor!" muttered Jackson. "Why, he's only a school boy. What does he know about business?"

"I think he has proved a match for you. Good-morning, Mr. Jackson. Ben, let us be going."

"Now," said Taylor as they were walking toward the inn, "what do you say to my offer?"

"Please state it, Mr. Taylor."

"I offer forty thousand dollars for the farm. It may be worth considerably more than that; but, on the other hand, the wells may soon run dry. I have to take the chances."

"That seems a fair offer, Mr. Taylor," said Ben frankly. "If I were the owner I would accept it; but I am acting for another who may not think as I do."

"Will you consult her and let me know?"

"I will write at once."

"Why not telegraph? The delay would be too great if you trust to the mail."

"I will do as you suggest," answered Ben, "if there is an opportunity to telegraph from this place."

"There is an office at the depot."

"Then I will take that on my way back to the hotel."

At one corner of the depot Ben found a telegraph operator. After a little consideration, he dashed off the following telegram:

> "No. - Madison Avenue, New York.
>
> "To Mrs. Hamilton:
>
> "Oil has been discovered on your farm. I am offered forty thousand dollars for it by a responsible party. What shall I do?
>
> "Ben Barclay."

"Send answer to the hotel," said Ben, to the operator.

Four hours later a messenger brought to Ben the following dispatch:

> "Your news is most surprising. Sell at the figure named if you think it best. You have full powers.
>
> "Helen Hamilton."

Mr. Taylor watched Ben's face eagerly as he read the telegram, for he knew that it must relate to his offer.

"What does your principal say?" he inquired.

"You can read the telegram, Mr. Taylor."

Taylor did so.

"So you have full powers?" he said. "Mrs. Hamilton must feel great confidence in you."

There was a proud flush on Ben's cheek as he replied:

"I have reason to think that she does. I hope it is not misplaced."

"I hope you won't drive a hard bargain with me, Ben."

"I don't mean to bargain at all. You have made a fair offer, and I will accept it."

Taylor looked pleased.

"Some boys in your position," he said, "would have stipulated for a present."

"I shall do nothing of the kind," said Ben promptly. "I should not think it honest."

"Your honesty, my boy, is of the old-fashioned kind. It is not the kind now in vogue. I like you the better for it, and if you were not in Mrs. Hamilton's employ I would try to secure your services myself."

"Thank you, Mr. Taylor. The time may come when

shall remind you of your promise."

"You will find I have not forgotten it. And now to business. We will go to a lawyer and have the necessary papers drawn up, which you shall sign in behalf of your principal."

The business was speedily arranged, and by suppertime Ben found that he had nothing further to detain him in Centerville. He felt that he had done a smart stroke of business. Mrs. Hamilton had been surprised at receiving an offer of five thousand dollars for the farm, yet he had sold it for forty thousand!

As they were returning from the lawyer's office they met farmer Jackson just returning from the post office.

"By the way, Mr. Jackson," said Taylor, "you will perhaps be interested to learn that your farm has been sold."

The farmer paused, and looked troubled.

"Are you going to turn me out of the house?" he asked.

"Not if you wish to live in it. I shall employ workmen at once to sink wells, and develop the property. They will need to board somewhere. Are you willing to board them?"

"Yes; I shall be glad to," answered Jackson. "I am a poor man, and it's hard work living by farming."

"Very well; we can no doubt make an arrangement. I am obliged to go to New York to complete arrangements for the transfer of the property, but I shall come back as soon as possible and commence operations."

"I wouldn't mind workin' for myself," said Jackson.

"Then you are the first man I engage."

The old farmer brightened up. He was to make money out of the new discoveries after all, though not in the way he had comtemplated.

"When are you going back to New York, Ben?" asked Taylor.

"There is nothing to detain me here any longer."

"We can go back together, then."

"I shall be glad to travel in your company, sir."

"Do you expect to remain in Mrs. Hamilton's employ?"

"I don't know," answered Ben.

"What were you doing?"

"Keeping accounts and acting as her private secretary."

"Do you like it?"

"Yes; I find it very pleasant, or would be but for one thing."

"What is that?"

"She has relatives living in the house who do not like me."

Horatio Alger, Jr.

"Jealous, eh?"

"Perhaps so."

"Let me say frankly, that you are fitted for something higher. I am a good judge of men - "

Ben smiled.

"Boys, then; and I consider you a boy of excellent business capacity. After I have got my oil wells under way, I should like to engage you as superintendent."

"I am flattered by your good opinion, Mr. Taylor, but it is a business I know nothing of."

"You would make it your business to learn it, or I mistake you."

"You are right there, sir."

"However, there will be plenty of time to arrange about this matter. It would probably be two months before I felt justified in leaving another in charge."

The two started for New York. About fifty miles before reaching the city, as Ben was reading a magazine he had purchased from the train-boy, he felt a touch upon his shoulder.

Looking up, he recognized, to his amazement, the tramp with whom he had had an adventure some weeks before in Pentonville.

"I see you know me," said the tramp, with a smile.

CHAPTER XXXIII

GOOD NEWS

The tramp, as we may call him for want of a different name, certainly showed signs of improvement in his personal appearance. He looked quite respectable, in fact, in a business suit of gray mixed cloth, and would have passed muster in any assemblage.

"I think I have met you before," answered Ben, with a smile.

"Perhaps it would have been more of a compliment not to have recognized me. I flatter myself that I have changed."

"So you have, and for the better."

"Thank you. I believe we rode together when we last met."

"Yes," said Ben.

"And you were not sorry to part copy with me - is it not so?"

"I won't contradict you."

Horatio Alger, Jr.

"Yet I am inclined to be your friend."

"I am glad of it," said Ben politely, though, truth to tell, he did not anticipate any particular benefit to accrue from the acquaintance of the speaker.

"I see you don't attach much importance to my offer of friendship. Yet I can do you an important service."

Mr. Taylor, who had been occupying a seat with Ben, here arose.

"You have something to say to my young friend," he said. "Take my seat."

"Don't let me deprive you of it," said the other with a politeness Ben had not deemed him capable of.

"By no means. I am going into the smoking car to smoke a cigar. Ben, I will be back soon."

"I didn't expect to meet you so far from Pentonville," said Ben's new companion, unable to suppress his curiosity.

"I don't live in Pentonville now."

"Where then?"

"In the city of New York."

"Are you employed there?"

"Yes; but I am just returning from a trip to Western Pennsylvania."

"Did you go on business?"

"Yes."

"Well, you are getting on, for a country boy. What do you hear from home?"

"My mother is well, but I fancy that is not what you mean."

"Yes, I am interested about your mother. Has she yet paid off that mortgage on her cottage?"

"How did you know there was a mortgage," asked Ben, in surprise.

"I know more than you suppose. What are the chances that she will be able to pay?"

"They are very small," answered Ben, gravely, "but the money is not yet due."

"When will it be due?"

"In about six weeks."

"Squire Davenport will foreclose - I know him well enough for that."

"So I suppose," said Ben, soberly.

"Is there no friend who will oblige you with the money?"

"I don't know of anyone I should feel at liberty to call on."

Horatio Alger, Jr.

It came into his mind that Mrs. Hamilton was abundantly able to help them, but she did not know his mother, and it would savor of presumption for him to ask so great a favor. True, he had effected a most profitable sale for her, but that was only in the line of his faithful duty, and gave him no claim upon his employer.

"I thought, perhaps, the gentlemen you were traveling with - the one who has gone info the smoking-car - might - "

"He is only a business acquaintance; I have known him less than a week."

"To be sure, that alters matters. He is not your employer, then?"

"No."

"Then I believe I shall have to help you myself."

Ben stared at his companion in amazement. What! this man who had robbed him of a dollar only four weeks before, to offer assistance in so important a matter!

"I suppose you are joking," said he, after a pause.

"Joking! Far from it. I mean just what I say. If Squire Davenport undertakes to deprive your mother of her home, I will interfere, and, you will see, with effect."

"Would you mind explaining to me how you would help us?" asked Ben.

"Yes, in confidence, it being understood that I follow

my own course in the matter."

"That is fair enough."

"Suppose I tell you, then, that Squire Davenport - I believe that is the title he goes by in your village - owes your mother more than the amount of the mortgage."

"Is this true?" said Ben, much surprised.

"It is quite true."

"But how can it be?"

"Your father, at his death, held a note of Davenport's for a thousand dollars - money which he had placed in his hands - a note bearing six per cent. interest."

Ben was more and more surprised; at first he was elated, then depressed.

"It will do me no good," he said, "nothing was found at father's death, and the note is no doubt destroyed."

"So Squire Davenport thinks," said his companion quietly.

"But isn't it true?"

"No; that note not only is in existence, but I knew where to lay my hands on it."

"Then it will more than offset the mortgage?" said Ben joyfully.

Horatio Alger, Jr.

"I should say. No interest has been paid on the note for more than five years. The amount due must be quite double the amount of the mortgage."

"How can I thank you for this information?" said Ben. "We shall not be forced to give up our little cottage, after all. But how could Squire Davenport so wickedly try to cheat us of our little property?"

"My dear boy," said the tramp, shrugging his shoulders, "your question savors of verdancy. Learn that there is no meanness too great to be inspired by the love of money."

"But Squire Davenport was already rich."

"And for that reason he desired to become richer."

"When shall we go to see the squire and tell him about the note?"

"I prefer that you should wait till the day the mortgage comes due. When is that?"

"On the twentieth of December."

"Then on the nineteenth of December we will both go to Pentonville and wait till the squire shows his hand."

"You seem to be - excuse me - in better circumstances than when we last met."

"I am. An old uncle of mine died last month, and considerately left me ten thousand dollars. Perhaps if he had known more about my way of life he would have found another heir. It has led me to turn over a new leaf, and henceforth I am respectable, as befits a man of property. I even keep a card case."

He drew out a card case and handed a card to Ben. It bore the name of Harvey Dinsmore.

"Mr. Dinsmore," said our young hero, I rejoice at your good fortune."

"Thank you. Shall we be friends?"

"With pleasure."

"Then I have more good news for you. Your father owned twenty-five shares in a Western railway. These shares are selling at par, and a year's dividends are due."

"Why, we shall be rich," said Ben, fairly dazzled by this second
stroke of good fortune.

"I hope so; though this is only a beginning."

"How can we prove that the railway shares belong to us?"

"Leave that to me. On the nineteenth of December you will meet me in Pentonville. Till then we probably shall not meet."

At this moment Mr. Taylor made his appearance, returning from the smoking-car, and Harvey Dinsmore left them.

"Well, Ben, has your friend entertained you?"

asked Taylor.

"He has told me some very good news."

"I am glad to hear it."

In due time they reached New York, and Ben started uptown to call upon Mrs. Hamilton.

CHAPTER XXXIV

CONRAD GOES INTO WALL STREET

When Conrad succeeded Ben as Mrs. Hamilton's private secretary, he was elated by what he considered his promotion. His first disappointment came when he learned that his salary was to be but five dollars a week. He did not dare to remonstrate with his employer, but he expressed himself freely to his mother.

"Cousin Hamilton might afford to pay me more than five dollars a week," he said bitterly.

"It is small," said his mother cautiously, "but we must look to the future."

"If you mean till Cousin Hamilton dies, it may be twenty or thirty years. Why, she looks healthier than you, mother, and will probably live longer."

Mrs. Hill looked grave. She did not fancy this speech.

"I don't think we shall have to wait so long," she said. "When you are twenty-one Cousin Hamilton will probably do something for you."

"That's almost five years," grumbled Conrad.

"At any rate we have got Ben Barclay out of the house, that's one comfort."

"Yes, I am glad of that; but I'd rather be in my old place than this, if I am to get only five dollars a week."

"Young people are so impatient," sighed Mrs. Hill. "You don't seem to consider that it isn't alone taking Ben's place, but you have got rid of a dangerous rival for the inheritance."

"That's true," said Conrad, "and I hated Ben. I'd rather any other boy would cut me out than he."

"Do you know what has become of him?"

"No; I expect that he has gone back to the country - unless he's blacking boots or selling papers downtown somewhere. By Jove, I'd like to come across him with a blacking-brush. He used to put on such airs. I would like to have heard Cousin Hamilton give him the grand bounce."

Nothing could be more untrue than that Ben putting on airs, but Conrad saw him through the eyes of prejudice, and persuaded himself that such was the fact. In reality Ben was exceedingly modest and unassuming, and it was this among other things that pleased Mrs. Hamilton.

Conrad continued to find his salary insufficient. He was still more dissatisfied after an interview with one of his school companions, a boy employed in a Wall Street broker's office.

He was just returning from an errand on which Mrs.

Hamilton had sent him, when he overtook Fred Lathrop on his way uptown.

The attention of Conrad was drawn to a heavy gold ring with a handsome stone on Fred's finger.

"Where did you get that ring?" asked Conrad, who had himself a fancy for rings.

"Bought it in Maiden Lane. How do you like it?"

"It is splendid. Do you mind telling me how much you paid?"

"I paid forty-five dollars. It's worth more."

"Forty-five dollars!" ejaculated Conrad. "Why, you must be a millionaire. Where did you get so much money?"

"I didn't find it in the street," answered Fred jocularly.

"Can't you tell a feller? You didn't save it out of your wages, did you?"

"My wages? I should say not. Why, I only get six dollars a week, and have to pay car fare and lunches out of that."

"Then it isn't equal to my five dollars, for that is all clear. But, all the same, I can't save anything."

"Nor I."

"Then how can you afford to buy forty-five dollar rings?"

"I don't mind telling you," said Fred. "I made the money by speculating."

"Speculating!" repeated Conrad, still in the dark.

"Yes. I'll tell you all about it."

"Do! there's a good fellow."

"You see, I bought fifty Erie shares on a margin."

"How's that?"

"Why I got a broker to buy me fifty shares on a margin of one per cent. He did it to oblige me. I hadn't any money to put up, but I had done him one or two favors, and he did it out of good nature. As the stock was on the rise, he didn't run much of a risk. Well, I bought at 44 and sold at 45 1-4. So I made fifty dollars over and above the commission. I tell you I felt good when the broker paid me over five ten-dollar bills."

"I should think you would."

"I was afraid I'd spend the money foolishly, so I went right off and bought this ring. I can sell it for what I gave any time."

Conrad's cupidity was greatly excited by this remarkable luck of Fred's.

"That seems an easy way of making money," he said. "Do you think I could try it?"

"Anybody can do it if he's got the money to plank down for a margin."

"I don't think I quite understand."

"Then I'll tell you. You buy fifty shares of stock, costing, say, fifty dollars a share."

"That would be twenty-five hundred dollars."

"Yes, if you bought it right out. But you don't. You give the broker whatever per cent. he requires, say a dollar a share - most of them don't do it so cheap - and he buys the stock on your account. If it goes up one or two points, say to fifty-one or fifty-two, he sells out, and the profit goes to you, deducting twenty-five cents a share which he charges for buying and selling. Besides that, he pays you back your margin."

"That's splendid. But doesn't it ever go down?"

"I should say so. If it goes down a dollar a share, then, of course, you lose fifty dollars."

Conrad looked serious. This was not quite so satisfactory.

"It is rather risky, then," he said.

"Of course, there's some risk; but you know the old proverb, 'Nothing venture, nothing have.' You must choose the right stock - one that is going up."

"I don't know anything about stock," said Conrad.

"I do," said Fred. "If I had money I know what I'd buy."

"What?" asked Conrad eagerly.

"Pacific Mail."

"Do you think that's going up?"

"I feel sure of it. I overheard my boss and another broker talking about it yesterday, and they both predicted a bull movement in it."

"Does that mean it's going up?"

"To be sure."

"I should like to buy some."

"Have you got money to plank down as a margin?"

Conrad had in his pocketbook fifty dollars which he had collected for Mrs. Hamilton, being a month's rent on a small store on Third Avenue. It flashed upon him that with this money he could make fifty dollars for himself, and be able to pay back the original sum to Mrs. Hamilton as soon as the operation was concluded.

"Could you manage it for me, Fred?" he asked.

"Yes, I wouldn't mind."

"Then I'll give you fifty dollars, and you do the best you can for me. If I succeed I'll make you a present."

"All right. I hope you'll win, I am sure [illegible]"

Not giving himself time to think of the serious breach of trust he was committing, Conrad took the money from his pocket and transferred it to his companion.

"It won't take long, will it?" he asked anxiously.

"Very likely the stock will be bought and sold to-morrow."

"That will be splendid. You'll let me know right off?"

"Yes; I'll attend to that."

Conrad went home and reported to Mrs. Hamilton that the tenant had not paid, but would do so on Saturday.

Mrs. Hamilton was a little surprised, for the Third Avenue tenant had never before put her off. Something in Conrad's manner excited her suspicion, and she resolved the next day to call herself on Mr. Clark, the tenant. He would be likely to speak of the postponement, and give reasons for it.

Horatio Alger, Jr.

CHAPTER XXXV

TURNING THE TABLES

"Now Conrad," said Mrs. Hamilton, "will you tell me by what authority you send away my visitors?"

"I didn't suppose you would want to see Ben," stammered Conrad.

"Why not?"

"After what he has done?"

"What has he done?"

"He stole your opera glass and pawned it."

"You are mistaken. It was stolen by a different person."

Conrad started uneasily, and his mother, who was not in the secret, looked surprised.

"I know who took the opera glass," continued Mrs. Hamilton.

"Who was it?" asked the housekeeper.

"Your son, I regret to say."

"This is a slander!" exclaimed Mrs. Hill angrily. "Cousin Hamilton, that boy has deceived you."

"My information did not come from Ben, if that is what you mean."

"My son would be incapable of stealing," continued Mrs. Hill.

"I should be glad to think so. It can easily be settled. Let Conrad go with me tomorrow to the pawnbroker from whom I recovered the glass, and see if he recognizes him."

"He would be sure to say it was me," stammered Conrad.

"At any rate he told me it was not Ben, who made no opposition to accompanying me."

"I see there is a plot against my poor boy," said Mrs. Hill bitterly.

"On the contrary, I shall be glad to believe him innocent. But there is another matter that requires investigation. Conrad, here is a letter which has come for you. Are you willing I should open and read it?"

"I don't like to show my letters," said Conrad sullenly.

"The boy is right," said his mother, always ready to back up her son.

"I have good reason for wishing to know the contents

Horatio Alger, Jr.

of the letter," said Mrs. Hamilton sternly. "I will not open it, unless Conrad consents, but I will call on the brokers and question them as to their motive in addressing it to a boy."

Conrad was silent. He saw that there was no escape for him.

"Shall I read it?" asked Mrs. Hamilton.

"Yes," answered Conrad feebly.

The letter was opened.

It ran thus:

> "Mr. Conrad Hill:
>
> "You will be kind enough to call at our office at once, and pay commission due us for buying add selling fifty shares Pacific Mail. The fall in the price of the stock, as we have already notified you, exhausted the money you placed in our hands as margin.
>
> > "Yours respectfully,"
> > "BIRD & BRANT."

"I hope, Cousin Hamilton, you won't be too hard on the poor boy," said the housekeeper. "He thought he would be able to replace the money."

"You and Conrad have done your best to prejudice me against Ben."

"You are mistaken," said the housekeeper quickly,

showing some evidence of agitation.

"I have learned that the letter which lured Ben to a gambling house was concocted between you. The letter I have in my possession."

"Who told you such a falsehood? If it is Ben - "

"It is not Ben, Mrs. Hill. He is as much surprised as you are to learn it now. The letter I submitted to an expert, who has positively identified the handwriting as yours, Mrs. Hill. You were very persistent in your attempts to make me believe than Ben was addicted to frequenting gambling houses."

"I see you are determined to believe me guilty," said Mrs. Hill. "Perhaps you think I know about the opera glass and this stock gambling?"

"I have no evidence of it, but I know enough to justify me in taking a decisive step."

Mrs. Hill listened apprehensively.

"It is this: you and Conrad must leave my house. I can no longer tolerate your presence here."

"You send us out to starve?" said the housekeeper bitterly.

"No; I will provide for you. I will allow you fifty dollars a month and Conrad half as much, and you can board where you please."

"While that boy usurps our place?" said Mrs. Hill bitterly.

"That is a matter to be decided between Ben and myself."

"We will go at once," said the housekeeper.

"I don't require it. You can stay here until you have secured a satisfactory boarding place."

But Conrad and his mother left the house the next morning. They saw that Mrs. Hamilton was no longer to be deceived, and they could gain nothing by staying. There was an angry scene between the mother and son.

"Were you mad, Conrad," said his mother, "to steal, where you were sure to be found out? It is your folly that has turned Cousin Hamilton against us?"

"No; it is that boy. I'd like to wring his neck!"

"I hope he will come to some bad end," said Mrs. Hill malignantly. "If he had not come to the house none of this would have happened."

Meanwhile Ben and his patroness had a satisfactory conversation.

"I hope you are satisfied with my management, Mrs. Hamilton?" said our hero.

"You have done wonderfully, Ben. Through you I am the richer by thirty-five thousand dollars at the very least, for the farm would have been dear at five thousand, whereas it was sold for forty thousand."

"I am very glad you are satisfied."

"You shall have reason to be glad. I intend to pay you a commission for selling the place."

"Thank you," said Ben joyfully.

He thought it possible Mrs. Hamilton might give him fifty dollars, and this would have been very welcome.

"Under the circumstances, I shall allow you an extra commission - say 10 per cent. How much will 10 per cent. amount to on forty thousand dollars?"

"Four thousand," answered Ben mechanically.

"Consider yourself worth fourth thousand dollars, then."

"But this is too much, Mrs. Hamilton," said Ben, scarcely crediting his good fortune.

"Then give half of it to your mother," said Mrs. Hamilton, smiling.

"Now we can pay off the mortgage!" exclaimed Ben, joyfully.

"What mortgage?"

Ben told the story, and it aroused the lively sympathy of his patroness.

"As soon as the purchase money is paid," she said, "you shall have you commission, and sooner if it is needed."

CHAPTER XXXVI

A LETTER FROM ROSE GARDINER

Ben resumed his place as the secretary and confidential clerk of Mrs. Hamilton. He found his position more agreeable when Mrs. Hill and Conrad were fairly out of the house. In place of the first a pleasant-faced German woman was engaged, and there were no more sour looks and sneering words.

Of course Ben kept up a weekly correspondence with his mother. He did not tell her the extent of his good fortune - he wished that to be a surprise, when the time came. From his mother, too, he received weekly letters, telling him not unfrequently how she missed him, though she was glad he was doing so well.

One day beside his mother's letter was another. He did not know the handwriting, but, looking eagerly to the end, he saw the name of Rose Gardiner.

"What would Rose say," Ben asked himself, "if she knew that I am worth four thousand dollars?"

The money had been paid to Ben, and was deposited in four different savings banks, till he could decide on a better investment. So he was quite sure of having more than enough to pay off the mortgage and redeem the cottage.

"Since mother is worrying, I must write and set her mind at rest," he decided.

He wrote accordingly, telling his mother not to feel anxious, for he had wealthy friends, and he felt sure, with their help, of paying off the mortgage. "But don't tell anybody this," he continued, "for I want to give the squire and Mr. Kirk a disagreeable surprise. I shall come to Pentonville two days before, and may stay a week."

He had already spoken to Mrs. Hamilton about having this week as a vacation.

Horatio Alger, Jr.

CHAPTER XXXVII

BEN'S VISIT TO PENTONVILLE

On the eighteenth of December Ben arrived in Pentonville. It was his first visit since he went up to New York for good. He reached home without observation, and found his mother overjoyed to see him.

"It has seemed a long, long time that you have been away, Ben," she said.

"Yes, mother; but I did a good thing in going to New York."

"You are looking well, Ben, and you have grown."

"Yes, mother; and best of all, I have prospered. Squire Davenport can't have the house!"

"You don't mean to say, Ben, that you have the money to pay it off?" asked his mother, with eager hope.

"Yes, mother; and, better still, the money is my own."

"This can't be true, Ben!" she said incredulously.

"Yes, but it is, though! You are to ask me no questions until after the twentieth. Then I will tell you all."

"I am afraid I shall have to send you to the store, for I am out of groceries."

A list was given, and Ben started for the store.

Mr. Kirk looked up in surprise as he entered.

"You're the Barclay boy, ain't you?"

"Yes, sir."

"I thought you were in New York."

"I was, but I have just got home."

"Couldn't make it, go, hey?"

Ben smiled, but did not answer.

"I may give you something to do," said Kirk, in a patronizing tone. "You've been employed in this store, I believe."

"Yes, I was here some months."

"I'll give you two dollars a week."

"Thank you," said Ben meekly, "but I shall have to take a little time to decide - say the rest of the week."

"I suppose you want to help your mother move?"

"She couldn't move alone."

"Very well; you can begin next Monday."

When Ben was going home, he met his old enemy, Tom Davenport. Tom's eyes lighted up when he saw Ben, and he crossed the street to speak to him. It may be mentioned that, though Ben had a new and stylish suit of clothes, he came home in the old suit he had worn away, and his appearance, therefore, by no means betokened prosperity.

"So you're back again!" said Tom abruptly.

"Yes."

"I always said you'd come back."

"Are you going to look for something to do?" Tom asked.

"Mr. Kirk has offered me a place in the store."

"How much pay?"

"Two dollars a week."

"You'd better take it."

"I hardly think I can work at that figure," said Ben, mildly.

"Kirk won't pay you any more."

"I'll think of it. By the way, Tom, call around and see me some time."

"I hardly think I shall have time," said Tom haughtily. "He talks as if I were his equal!" he said to himself.

"Well, good afternoon. Remember me to your father."

Tom stared at Ben in surprise. Really the store boy was getting very presumptuous he thought.

CHAPTER XXXVIII

CONCLUSION

On the evening of the nineteenth of December, Ben stood on the piazza of the village hotel when the stage returned from the depot. He examined anxiously the passengers who got out. His eyes lighted up joyfully as he recognized in one the man he was looking for.

"Mr. Dinsmore," he said, coming forward hastily.

"You see I have kept my word," said Harvey Dinsmore, with a smile.

"I feared you would not come."

"I wished to see the discomfiture of our friend Squire Davenport. So to-morrow is the day?"

"Yes."

"I should like to be on hand when the squire calls."

"That will be at twelve o'clock. My mother has received a note from him fixing that hour."

"Then I will come over at half-past eleven if you will allow me."

"Come; we will expect you."

"And how have you fared since I saw you, my young friend?"

"I have been wonderfully fortunate, but I have kept my good fortune a secret from all, even my mother. It will come out to-morrow."

"Your mother can feel quite at ease about the mortgage."

"Yes, even if you had not come I am able to pay it."

"Whew! then you have indeed been fortunate for a boy. I suppose you borrowed the money?"

"No; I earned it."

"Evidently you were born to succeed. Will you take supper with me?"

"Thank you. Mother will expect me at home."

At half-past eleven the next forenoon the stranger called at door of Mrs. Barclay. He was admitted by Ben.

"Mother," said Ben, "this is Mr. Harvey Dinsmore."

"I believe we have met before," said Dinsmore, smiling. "I fear my first visit was not welcome. To-day I come in more respectable guise and as a friend."

"You are welcome, sir," said the widow courteously. "I am glad to see you. I should hardly have known you."

"I take that as a compliment. I am a tramp no longer, but a respectable and, I may add, well-to-do citizen. Now I have a favor to ask."

"Name it, sir."

"Place me, if convenient, where I can hear the interview between Mr. Davenport and yourself without myself being seen."

Ben conducted Dinsmore into the kitchen opening out of the sitting room, and gave him a chair.

At five minute to twelve there was a knock at the outer door, and Ben admitted Squire Davenport.

"So you are home again, Benjamin," said the squire. "Had enough of the city?"

"I am taking a vacation. I thought mother would need me to-day."

"She will - to help her move."

"Step in, sir."

Squire Davenport, with the air of a master, followed Ben into the sitting room. Mrs. Barclay sat quietly at the table with her sewing in hand.

"Good-day, widow," said the squire patronizingly.

He was rather surprised at her quiet, unruffled, demeanor. He expected to find her tearful and sad.

"Good-day, Squire Davenport," she said quietly. "Is

your family well?"

"Zounds! she takes it coolly," thought the squire.

"Very well," he said dryly. "I suppose you know my business?"

"You come about the mortgage?"

"Yes; have you decided where to move?"

"My mother does not propose to move," said Ben calmly.

"Oho! that's your opinion, is it? I apprehend it is not for you to say."

"That's where we differ. We intend to stay."

"Without consulting me, eh?"

"Yes, sir."

"You are impudent, boy!" said the squire, waxing wrathful. "I shall give you just three days to find another home, though I could force you to leave at once."

"This house belongs to my mother."

"You are mistaken. It belongs to me."

"When did you buy it?"

"You are talking foolishly. I hold a mortgage for seven hundred dollars on the property, and you can't pay it. I am willing to cancel the mortgage and pay your mother three hundred dollars cash for the place."

"It is worth a good deal more."

"Who will pay more?" demanded the quire, throwing himself back in his chair.

"I will," answered Ben.

"Ho, ho! that's a good joke," said the squire. "Why, you are notworth five dollars in the world."

"It doesn't matter whether I am or not. My mother won't sell."

"Then pay the mortgage," said the squire angrily.

"I am prepared to do so. Have you a release with you?"

Squire Davenport stared at Ben in amazement.

"Enough of this folly!" he said sternly. I am not in the humor for jokes."

"Squire Davenport, I am not joking. I have here money enough to pay the mortgage," and Ben drew from his pocket a thick roll of bills.

"Where did you get that money?" asked Squire Davenport, in evident discomfiture.

"I don't think it necessary to answer that question; but there is another matter I wish to speak to you about. When will you be ready to pay the sum you owe my father's estate?"

Squire Davenport started violently.

"What do you mean?" he demanded hoarsely.

Harvey Dinsmore entered the room from the kitchen at that point.

"I will answer that question," he said. "Ben refers to a note for a thousand dollars signed by you, which was found on his father's person at the time of his death."

"No such note is in existence," said the squire triumphantly. He remembered that he had burned it.

"You are mistaken. That note you burned was only a copy! I have the original with me."

"You treacherous rascal!" exclaimed the squire, in great excitement.

"When I have dealings with a knave I am not very scrupulous," said Dinsmore coolly.

"I won't pay the note you have trumped up. This is a conspiracy."

"Then," said Ben, "the note will be placed in the hands of a lawyer."

"This is a conspiracy to prevent my foreclosing the mortgage. But it won't work," said the squire angrily.

"There you are mistaken. I will pay the mortgage now in the presence of Mr. Dinsmore, and let the other matter be settled hereafter. Please prepare the necessary papers."

Suddenly the squire did as requested. The money was paid over, and Ben, turning to his mother, said:

"Mother, the house is ours once more without incumbrance."

"Thank God!" ejaculated the widow.

"Mr. Dinsmore," said Squire Davenport, when the business was concluded, "may I have a private word with you? Please accompany me to my house."

"As you please, sir."

When they emerged into the street Squire Davenport said:

"Of course this is all a humbug. You can't have the original with you?"

"But I have, sir. You should have looked more closely at the one you burned."

"Can't we compromise this matter?" asked the squire, in an insinuating tone.

"No sir," said Dinsmore with emphasis. "I have got through with rascality. You can't tempt me. If I were as hard up as when I called upon you before, I might not be able to resist you; but I am worth over ten thousand dollars, and - "

"Have you broken into a bank?" asked Squire Davenport, with a sneer.

"I have come into a legacy. To cut matters short, it will

be for your interest to pay this claim, and not allow the story to be made known. It would damage your reputation."

In the end this was what the squire was forced very unwillingly to do. The amount he had to pay to the estate of the man whose family he had sought to defraud was nearly fifteen hundred dollars. This, added to Ben's four thousand, made the family very comfortable. Mr. Kirk was compelled to look elsewhere for a house. No one was more chagrined at the unexpected issue of the affair than Tom Davenport, whose mean and jealous disposition made more intense his hatred of Ben.

*　*　*　*　*　*　*　*　*

Several years have elapsed. Ben is in the office of a real estate lawyer in New York, as junior partner. All Mrs. Hamilton's business is in his hands, and it is generally thought that he will receive a handsome legacy from her eventually. Mrs. Barclay prefers to live in Pentonville, but Ben often visits her. Whenever he goes to Pentonville he never fails to call on Rose Gardiner, now a beautiful young lady of marriageable age. She has lost none of her partiality for Ben, and it is generally understood that they are engaged. I have reason to think that the rumor is correct and that Rose will change her name to Barclay within a year. Nothing could be more agreeable to Mrs. Barclay, who has long looked upon Rose as a daughter.

Tom Davenport is now in the city, but his course is far from creditable. His father has more than once been compelled to pay his debts, and has angrily refused to do so again. In fact, he has lost a large part of his once handsome fortune, and bids fair to close his life in penury. Success has come to Ben because he deserved it, and well-merited retribution to Tom Davenport. Harvey Dinsmore, once given over to evil courses, has redeemed himself, and is a reputable business man in New York. Mrs. Hamilton still lives, happy in the success of her protege. Conrad and his mother have tried more than once to regain their positions in her household, but in vain. None of my young readers will pity them. They are fully rewarded for their treachery.